5/09

Including**Alice**

Books by Phyllis Reynolds Naylor

○–○–○–○–○–○–○–○

Witch's Sister
Witch Water
The Witch Herself
Walking Through the Dark
How I Came to Be a Writer
How Lazy Can You Get?
Eddie, Incorporated
All Because I'm Older
Shadows on the Wall
Faces in the Water
Footprints at the Window
The Boy with the Helium Head
A String of Chances
The Solomon System
Bernie Magruder and the Case of the Big Stink
Night Cry
Old Sadie and the Christmas Bear
The Dark of the Tunnel
The Agony of Alice
The Keeper
Bernie Magruder and the Disappearing Bodies
The Year of the Gopher
Beetles, Lightly Toasted
Maudie in the Middle
One of the Third Grade Thonkers
Alice in Rapture, Sort Of
Keeping a Christmas Secret
Bernie Magruder and the Haunted Hotel
Send No Blessings
Reluctantly Alice
King of the Playground
Shiloh

Including**Alice**

PHYLLIS REYNOLDS NAYLOR

Atheneum Books for Young Readers
NEW YORK • LONDON • TORONTO • SYDNEY

DISCARD

Atheneum Books for Young Readers
An imprint of Simon & Schuster
Children's Publishing Division
1230 Avenue of the Americas
New York, New York 10020

The poem on page 260, "Passing By," was
written by Thomas Ford (1580–1648).

Book design by Ann Sullivan
The text for this book is set in Berkeley Old Style.
Manufactured in the United States of America
First Edition
2 4 6 8 10 9 7 5 3 1
Library of Congress Cataloging-in-Publication Data
Naylor, Phyllis Reynolds.
Including Alice / Phyllis Reynolds Naylor.—1st ed.
p.   cm.
Summary: Fifteen-year-old Alice finds it hard to
adjust to the changes in her life when her father gets
married and her brother moves to his own apartment.
ISBN 0-689-82637-0
[1. Remarriage—Fiction. 2. Interpersonal relations—Fiction.
3. Self-confidence—Fiction. 4. High schools—Fiction.
5. Schools—Fiction.] I. Title.
PZ7 .N24In 2004
[Fic]—dc22   2003018210

To Catherine Wood,
my role model, and

With special thanks to Martin Small
for his Piano Trio no. 2

Contents

Getting Ready

I didn't know you could be excited and scared and happy and sad all at the same time, but that's how I started my sophomore year.

Happy because: Dad and Sylvia had set the date and would be married October 18.

Scared because: ditto. I was getting a stepmom, and I wanted things to be perfect.

Sad because: Lester had moved out.

Excited because: ditto. He was now living in a bachelor apartment a couple of miles away with two other guys, and he said I could visit him there.

Dad was already using Lester's old bedroom as an office, keeping the twin bed as a couch so Lester could come home for a night if he wanted. I wondered what kind of a bed my brother would buy for his new place—a bed for one person or two?

"So?" I said when he stopped by to pick up

another load of books. "What kind of bed did you buy, Lester? Twin or double?"

"Oh, I was thinking about one of those king-size circular numbers on a rotating base with a mirrored ceiling and a stereo in the headboard," he said.

I punched his arm and laughed. Everything seemed to be changing so fast, though, and all at the same time—Lester's moving, the start of school, the coming wedding. . . . We hadn't even celebrated Lester's twenty-third birthday properly. I'd just sent him a card with a certificate for a free car wash at the Autoclean.

I was feeling giddy with the "rush of life," as Aunt Sally would call it, as though I were being swept downstream by a fast-moving current, ready or not.

What I was most nervous about was that in a few weeks I'd be living here with Dad and a new mother without Lester around. Always before, I had imagined him cracking jokes at the dinner table and making Sylvia laugh. I imagined how funny it would be if he forgot and came to breakfast some morning in his boxer shorts. I imagined the four of us cooking dinner together or watching a football game on TV—Lester being here for all our celebrations.

Now, if Dad wasn't here and Lester was gone,

what would I *talk* about to the woman who used to be my seventh-grade English teacher? What if I said *me* instead of *I* or *lay* instead of *lie*? Who got to shower first in the morning, and what if I forgot to wipe out the sink after I'd used it?

Lester was rummaging through the refrigerator at the moment, looking for leftovers he could take back to his apartment for lunch. Suddenly I reached out and circled him with my arms, my head against his back. "I'm going to miss you," I said, and swallowed.

"Hey!" he said over his shoulder, patting my hand. "The food will never be as good there as it is here. There's an umbilical cord that stretches between me and this refrigerator, don't you worry."

Assignments were piling up on me at school, so I couldn't think about the wedding 24/7. I'd squeaked by with a C– in Algebra I last year, and now I was wrestling with Algebra II. Next year it would be geometry and the year after that, physics. And since Patrick Long, the genius, was my *ex*-boyfriend, I was counting on Gwen Wheeler to get me through.

Gwen and Elizabeth and Pamela are my three closest friends, and we're so different. Like the different things that make up a salad, I guess, we go well together. We'd all been assistant counselors at a camp the summer before, and that had made us closer still.

Now we were eating lunch out on the school steps, and the September sun felt delicious on my neck and arms. My thighs were toasty inside my jeans.

"Aren't you *excited* about the wedding, Alice?" Elizabeth asked. She looked gorgeous in a cobalt blue top and black pants. Elizabeth, with her dark hair and eyelashes, looks good in practically anything she puts on. "It's like you brought them together. This wouldn't be happening if it weren't for you."

"I know," I said. "But we've waited so long for this, I'll believe it when I hear them say 'I do.'"

First we'd waited for Sylvia to decide between Dad and her old boyfriend, Jim Sorringer. Then she was an exchange teacher in England, and *then* her sister Nancy got sick and the wedding was postponed. Sylvia had gone out west during the summer to be with Nancy. She had even taken a leave of absence from teaching for September and October, in case Nancy grew worse. But her sister was recovering, Sylvia was due to come home on October 1, and all systems were go. I could stop worrying, I told myself.

Elizabeth, though, looked thoughtful. "Wouldn't

it be dramatic if right before the minister pronounced them man and wife, Jim Sorringer stood
up at the back of the church and said he couldn't
live without her?"

"Don't even *think* it!" I warned, hoping that our
vice principal back in junior high would stay as far
away from the wedding as possible.

Pamela grinned as she lifted the top half of her
bun, removed the pickle, and closed her hamburger up again. "It would be even more dramatic
if he announced that he had loved her first and was
suing your dad for alienating her affections. You
should bar Jim Sorringer from the wedding, Alice."

"Stop it, you guys! I'm wired enough as it is!" I
said.

Gwen laughed. Her laugh is like warm syrup,
and her skin is the color of Log Cabin maple. "I
think you should bar *Liz* and *Pam* from the wedding, Alice. They'll sit there and cry and make a
scene."

"No, we won't!" said Elizabeth. "We'll be looking at Lester. He'll be gorgeous in a tuxedo."

"He and Dad aren't wearing tuxedos. They're
wearing suits," I announced.

"Not wearing *tuxedos*!" Elizabeth said.

"Doesn't matter. Les would be gorgeous without
anything at all!" said Pamela. "*Especially* without
anything at all, and you can tell him I said so."

Elizabeth Price and Pamela Jones have been crazy about my brother ever since we moved to Silver Spring four years ago. And now that Lester's in graduate school and in an apartment, they've been driving me nuts to go over and see him.

"I think it's time we met his roommates," said Pamela.

"Yes! Why don't we surprise them and take over dinner some night?" Elizabeth suggested. "We could cook it ourselves."

"You can't just walk in on a bunch of guys like that," Gwen said as the bell rang and she gathered up her books.

"Why not?" I asked, sort of liking the idea. "Lester doesn't call ahead when *he's* dropping by."

Gwen rolled her eyes and shrugged. "You just *can't!*" she said, and went inside the double doors.

There's a new girl in my gym class this year. I remember how awkward it feels to start school in a new place where you don't know a single person. I know the drill—how you smile to show others you're friendly and approachable, but you don't impose yourself on anyone, and you try to make friends one at a time until someone invites you to join the group.

But Amy Sheldon doesn't do that. It's like she looks the whole scene over, decides where she wants to belong, and then walks over and barges in. No subtlety whatsoever. I hate to say it, but maybe if she were cute, we'd think it was funny, I don't know. Some girls are naturally hot, like Elizabeth, and some girls are naturally not. Amy, unfortunately, is not. She has a long narrow face, with eyes that come too close together, and there's a wide space between her nose and upper lip. But it's what happens when Amy opens her mouth that turns us off. She keeps coming up with comments that don't quite fit.

For example, somebody might say, "I've got this itch behind my knee that's driving me crazy!" and Amy will say, "I had chicken pox when I was five." And we just look at her, not knowing if Amy responds the way she does because she's a little slow or because her mind is actually galloping on ahead of us, computing the itch, the rash, the diseases that cause a rash, and all the assorted illnesses of childhood. Sometimes she laughs at things no one else thinks are funny, and other times she doesn't get it when someone tells a joke. She's just . . . well . . . Amy. And she wants so much to fit in—*some*where!

"I hear your dad's getting married," she commented as we came out of the showers, our towels wrapped around us.

"Yeah, in a couple of weeks," I said.

"Am I invited?" she asked. Just like that.

"Oh, wow!" I said. "I wish we could invite the whole school, but of course we can't."

That got me thinking, though, that all my friends probably assumed they could come to the wedding. Dad and Sylvia had told me I could invite three friends to the reception, and I'd given them the names of Elizabeth, Pamela, and Gwen. But what about the ceremony at the church on Cedar Lane?

At dinner that night, just Dad and me and two pork chops, I said, "I know I can only have three friends at the reception, but how many can I invite to the wedding?"

Dad paused with a forkful of green beans balanced above his plate. "I don't know that much about wedding etiquette, Al, but I don't think you can invite people to the ceremony and then not let them come to the reception. And that guest list is out of control."

"How many are coming to the reception?" I asked.

"Sixty and counting," Dad said.

"I thought you and Sylvia wanted a small wedding—just family and friends," I reminded him. "So who *are* all these people?"

"Sylvia's teacher friends at school, plus their spouses or sweethearts; my employees and

instructors from the Melody Inn, plus *their* significant others; a few of my customers; old childhood
friends of Sylvia's; your three friends; and all our
relatives. We can't squeeze in another person."

"You mean none of my other friends can see you
guys get married?" I asked incredulously.

"Al, how do we drive off to the reception after
the ceremony and leave half the guests behind?"
he said.

"Dad!" I wailed. "I've told all my friends about
your engagement! Everyone at school has been
hearing me talk about this for months! For years!"
My eyes filled with tears. I *hate* that! I hate that I'm
fifteen years old and I still cry when I get upset.

"Look, I'll talk to Sylvia," Dad said quickly. "I
know we can't have any more people at the reception, but I'll see what I can work out at the
church."

Inwardly, I had to admit that I'd fantasized about
everyone I know watching me walk down the aisle
ahead of Sylvia in my teal bridesmaid dress with
the thin straps. I imagined them watching me take
my place across from Dad and Lester, my eyes on
Sylvia, but all of my friends' eyes on me.

I stayed off e-mail that evening and didn't use
the phone, either. I didn't want to say one word to
one more person about the wedding and then find
out I'd have to un-invite everyone.

When the phone rang later, Dad answered, and finally he stopped in the doorway of my room, where I was working on a history assignment.

"Sylvia says that of course your other friends are invited to the ceremony, Alice. She said we'll order some punch and cookies there in the church lounge for people from school who would like to attend."

Life was looking up. "How many can I invite?" I asked, thinking of the whole sophomore class.

"Oh, I don't know. Five, maybe?"

"*Five?*" I shrieked. "Dad, it has to be at least fifteen!"

"Sylvia thinks other students from her junior high school may drop in unannounced, Alice, and the sanctuary just isn't that big. We don't want this to turn into a circus. Let's compromise: ten, max. *Including* Elizabeth, Pamela, and Gwen."

When Dad went back downstairs, I wrote the numbers 1 to 10 on a sheet of paper and put a name beside each number:

1. Elizabeth
2. Pamela
3. Gwen
4. Patrick
5. Lori
6. Karen

7. Jill
8. Mark
9. Brian
10. Justin

These are the friends I've known the longest. I could have included Donald Sheavers, my friend back in Takoma Park, but he didn't know Sylvia. I could have included Leslie, Lori's girlfriend, and Faith and Molly from the high school stage crew, and some of my friends on the newspaper staff, but they didn't know Sylvia either. The one person I was sure I would *not* invite was Penny, the girl who had caused the breakup between Patrick and me.

I heard Lester come in later to talk with Dad about some problem he was having with his car. So I took the opportunity to work on the wedding gift I was making for Dad and Sylvia. I'd wanted it to be something I made with my own hands, because those are the kinds of presents that Dad likes most.

I'd bought a set of white percale sheets and pillowcases, and I'd gotten this really fancy monogram pattern with an *M* in the middle, a *B* (for *Ben*) on one side, and an *S* (for *Sylvia*) on the other, with flowers and doves forming a circular border. It looked great on the pattern, and I'd finally gotten the outline transferred to each pillowcase and in the center of one hem of the unfitted sheet. All I had to do was embroider it.

The *M* would be embroidered with teal-colored thread, Sylvia's favorite color. The *B* and the *S* would be royal blue, her other color for her wedding, and the flowers and doves would be shades of green and gold. It was going to be beautiful, but I wasn't very good at sewing and it seemed I took out a stitch for every two I put in. I hadn't realized I had to make stitches so tiny. So far all I'd got done was the *M* and the *B* and half of the *S,* plus one dove on just one of the pillowcases. I didn't know how I was going to finish in time for the wedding. Each night I tried to put in a half hour on it before I went to bed, but it wasn't easy to find time when Dad wasn't around.

I heard someone coming upstairs and quickly put the sheet away, but it was Lester coming to say hi to me. I asked what *he* was giving Dad and Sylvia for their wedding.

"I gave up my room, didn't I?" he said.

"That's *all*?" I asked. Lester has teased me for so long, it's hard to know when he's serious.

He laughed. "Actually, I found a clock. The face is embedded in burled wood, and the grain's absolutely gorgeous. They can put it anywhere they like, but if it were mine, I'd set it on the mantel. We've never had a decent clock in this house. They all look like they came from Sears."

"It sounds great," I said, wondering how my embroidered sheets and pillowcases would look compared to that. I also wondered what Lester's apartment looked like now that all three guys had moved in. The furniture was all chrome and glass, I'll bet.

"Pamela wants to know when she can come over and visit you," I said. "Elizabeth, too."

"Hmm," said Lester. "I'll have to check my social calendar. Two . . . three years, maybe."

"Lester!"

He grinned.

"They want to meet your roommates," I told him. "Are they studly? Pamela wants to know."

"Ugly as trolls," Lester said. "One's got warts all over his face, and the other's got a third ear."

Now it was my turn to grin. "Elizabeth can't wait for the wedding. She wants to see you in a three-piece suit, and Pamela wants to see you without anything on at all."

"Make that ten years before they can visit me," Lester said.

Just before homeroom the next day Karen told me something she'd just heard—that Penny had asked Patrick out. You can't believe half of what Karen says because her day isn't complete unless she riles somebody up. Karen has a lot of good points, but discretion isn't one of them.

"So?" I said, putting my jacket in my locker. "It's a free country." They'd broken up months ago, but, I suppose, like Patrick and me, they were still friends. "Why are you telling *me* this?"

"Well . . . I just thought you should know . . . because it's the day your dad's getting married," Karen said, wincing a little.

Now I was mad. I was steamed. I was furious. I had saved one of my ten precious slots for Patrick, and she'd asked him out? She *knew* that was the day my dad was getting married. Maybe I didn't want Patrick again for my boyfriend, but I wanted him to *see* me in my bridesmaid dress! I wanted him to watch me come down the aisle. I wanted to see *him* all dressed up, smiling at me at a wedding.

"So?" I said again, trying not to show just how upset I was. "Did Patrick say yes or what?"

"I don't know," Karen said.

I had planned to e-mail the seven new people I was inviting to the ceremony when I got home that afternoon, but now I was determined to invite them in the cafeteria the next day. Since

Penny usually sat with us, it would be much too obvious if I called out ten names and hers wasn't one of them, but I was going to make sure she knew she was excluded. Let *her* see how it felt to be unwanted. Let *her* get a taste of being odd man out.

I guess I had never fully admitted to myself how angry I was at her for stealing Patrick away from me. Even though it was Patrick's decision as much as it was hers. Even though they weren't even going out together anymore. I never wanted her to know how much that had hurt me. But now I was surprised at how strangely satisfying it felt to know I could exclude her from the wedding.

So after I finished my egg salad at lunch that day, I got up and casually moved around both tables— we always push two together—whispering the invitation, the time and place, adding that they were invited to stay for punch and cookies afterward.

Even though I told Jill about the invitation when Penny was talking to Mark, and I told Mark when Penny had turned to Jill, Penny could sense that something was up and looked quizzically around the table. She glanced my way then, and I, Miss Innocent, laughed a little too loudly at a joke Brian just told, ignoring her. Totally. I can't say that my dad's wedding was making me a better person exactly, but I'd have to admit it gave me a lot of pleasure.

The thing was, Amy Sheldon had been sitting at a table next to ours, and she must have overheard me say something about the wedding. Because she got right up from her chair and came over.

"Alice," she said, "am I invited now?"

I couldn't believe she asked me outright like that, even though I'd told her before that she wasn't. And because I figured that at least one of my ten friends wouldn't be able to make it, and because I knew that Penny was listening—okay, *especially* because I knew she was listening—I said, "Sure, Amy, we have room for exactly one more, and you're it."

Penny looked away then and gathered up her books. I should have felt bad I'd hurt her feelings, but I didn't feel sorry in the least.

2

Mixed Feelings

Sylvia was back, and I was discovering just how much work there was to planning a wedding. You not only have to find a cake and a photographer and musicians and a dressmaker and a florist; you have to find hotel rooms for all the guests coming from out of town.

I guess we're sort of short on relatives. My mom's parents died a long time ago, and so did Dad's mother. But Uncle Harold and Uncle Howard were driving up from Tennessee with their wives and were bringing Grandpa McKinley with them. Aunt Sally and Uncle Milt were flying in from Chicago, along with their daughter Carol, who's a few years older than Lester. Sylvia's sister was coming, of course, and so was her brother and his family from Seattle. They all needed places to stay. There were now lists taped all over our house—to cabinet doors and mirrors and walls—

hotel numbers, airline numbers, taxi service, car rental. . . .

"I'd forgotten you have a brother," I said to Sylvia as she posted his flight information above our phone one night when she came for dinner. "I never hear you talk about him much."

"Kirk? No, I guess I don't. I was always closer to Nancy, I think." She paused a minute. "I've always envied your closeness with Lester."

I wondered if I had heard right. Sylvia envied *me*?

"How come you weren't closer?" I asked. "Or is that personal?"

"Maybe because there's a five-year difference in age between Kirk and me, while there's only two years between Nancy and me," she said.

"Is he older or younger than you?"

"Older," she said, and added ruefully, "and always treated me like I didn't have a brain in my head." She sighed. "Actually, our falling out was over politics. We'll never see eye to eye on that, and we've sort of agreed to disagree. But he's very active politically, so there hasn't been a whole lot to talk about, it seems. He's married, I'm not; he has children, I don't—that sort of thing. Maybe now we'll feel closer."

Wow! I thought. Lester and I *never* discuss politics, but we talk about all kinds of other things.

"Is he going to be in the wedding?" I asked.

She laughed. "Oh, yes. I asked him if he wanted to give the bride away, and he said, 'Gladly!'" I laughed too. Then she added, "I think it was Nancy's being sick that helped bring us together again. All the while I was in Albuquerque taking care of her, Kirk called every day and flew down there twice. Sometimes it takes something serious to make you realize what's important. Kirk told me I could vote for Mickey Mouse after that, and he still wouldn't hold it against me. So maybe that old saying's right—you know, about something good coming out of something bad."

I had a thought just then that I didn't even put into words: The worst thing that had ever happened to me was losing my mother. Would the nicest thing that ever happened be that I got Sylvia for a stepmom? And my mother had to die for that to happen?

Ten days before the wedding Sylvia called us before Dad went to work, and I answered. "I'm going to be picking up your gown in Bethesda this afternoon," she said. "There's a really great restaurant over there on Norfolk Avenue," and she gave me the address. "Why don't you and Ben meet me there for dinner, and we'll have a quiet, relaxed meal, just the three of us, before all the wedding craziness takes over."

"Sure!" I said.

At six o'clock Dad and I met her in Bethesda. I put on my best top and necklace because I wanted to show Sylvia that I could be a daughter she was proud of in public, and we had a great seafood dinner, except that one of my sleeves dragged in the tartar sauce.

Sylvia caught me trying to clean it off with a napkin I'd dipped in my water glass. She grinned. "It happens," she said. Mellow, that's what she is. I'll bet I could have dumped my whole dinner in my lap and she would have just smiled.

We drove back to our house in two cars. I rode with Sylvia, her backseat full of purchases, including my dress. After we got it upstairs, Sylvia handed me a small bag. "I took a chance on your size and bought you a strapless bra," she said.

I squealed when I saw VICTORIA'S SECRET printed on the bag. I'd never had anything from there. But it was the dress with the thin straps that made me gasp. Even though she'd let me choose the style, it was more beautiful than I'd imagined.

"It's so gorgeous!" I told her. "I'm going to wear it to the senior prom!"

She laughed. "Well, that's half your problem solved, then!" and I suppose she meant that finding a date was the other half.

I doubted Sylvia Summers had ever had a problem getting a date. She has light brown hair and blue eyes, great cheekbones, and a medium-size figure. Five feet six, I'd guess—maybe 130 pounds. She doesn't look like a half-starved prisoner of war, as Lester calls the supermodels. I'd never met her sister, but I wondered if she looked anything like Sylvia.

"Was Nancy ever married?" I asked as I carefully hung my dress in the closet.

"Once. They divorced," Sylvia told me. "I was never quite sure what the problem was. She just said they grew apart, but I suppose that could mean a number of things. In any case, she seems happy being single."

"Has she decided whether or not to be in the wedding?" I wanted to know. "Is she okay now?"

"Not completely okay, but so much better. She's still weak, but she's bringing her dress along with her, even if she decides not to be part of the ceremony."

My first thought, of course, was that if Nancy wasn't in the wedding as maid of honor, then I would take her place. But I saw that Sylvia was opening another box on my bed, and she winked at me.

"Help me try this on," she said. "Just to see how it will look."

There was the bridal veil and then the headpiece,

a delicate wire frame with floating pearls on it.

She sat down on the edge of my bed, and I lifted the veil in my hands. It was as though I were being admitted into the inner sanctum. As though I had suddenly got to be twenty-one. As though I were Sylvia's sister, not her stepdaughter-to-be. I carefully arranged the long veil over Sylvia's hair and placed the headpiece on top of that. The pearls appeared to be scattered here and there in Sylvia's light brown hair. We studied the effect in the mirror.

"It's beautiful!" I said. "*You're* beautiful!"

"Right now I think I'm the luckiest woman alive!" she answered.

We heard Dad shuffling around in the hall. "So what's taking so long in there?" he called, and we giggled and placed the veil back in the box so he wouldn't see it till the wedding day.

"Nothing," I called when the lid was on the box. "You can come in now."

The way his eyes lit up when he looked at her, even without the veil, made me wonder if he'd ever looked at my mom like that. He *must* have. I'd just been too young to notice.

"So how are my girls doing?" Dad asked.

"*Women!*" Sylvia corrected in mock seriousness, and I glanced in the mirror to see if I still looked as elegant as I had at dinner. Maybe I *did* look older these days. My hair was certainly getting darker. I used to think of myself as a strawberry blonde, but I was looking more brunette every day. And there was hardly any "baby fat" left under my chin.

"I'm getting lonely downstairs," Dad told Sylvia, taking her hand. "We've still got a lot to talk about."

After she left, I peeked into the Victoria's Secret bag. There was a white strapless bra, the top half all lace. Sylvia was a good judge of size: I tried it on and it fit well. *Sexy!* I thought, and giggled. *A real hottie!* Too bad no one would see it but me.

Dad and Sylvia were having coffee at the dining-room table when I went down. I settled myself in the living room to read a chapter from my literature book. Little wisps of conversation came to me now and then as they went over their checklists.

"I settled with the photographer on the number of prints, one set for each relative. . . ."

"Martin's going to bring the musicians over some evening and let me hear his trio. . . ."

"I know Nancy wants desperately to be in the wedding, but she just has no stamina. . . ."

After a while I went out in the kitchen to get some sherbet for myself, and as I was dishing it up I heard Sylvia say something about "the addition" and whether the tub should be a Jacuzzi.

"What's this?" I asked, going to the doorway.

"Daydreaming," Sylvia said.

"We've been toying with the idea of an addition on the back of the house," said Dad.

"Really?"

"It might be nice to enlarge our bedroom, add a bath on the upper level, with a study below next to the dining room," said Sylvia.

I gave my head a little shake to clear it. Weren't there enough changes right now without changing the house too? After all, it *was* my house as well.

"Which means, of course, that you'd have our present bathroom all to yourself," Dad said.

"I thought you were going to use Lester's room for a study," I told him.

"It's okay for now, but it's not nearly big enough for both Sylvia's things and mine. She has lessons to plan, I have records to keep. We'd turn Lester's room into a guest room so that there was always a place for company. What do you think?"

What *could* I think? They'd already decided on it, obviously.

Sylvia went right on talking to Dad: "You can get a standard tub with a Jacuzzi too. That way we won't be using extra water to fill it when we only want a bath."

"Now, that's a practical idea," Dad said. And

they continued talking as if I weren't even there. I began to feel like Amy Sheldon, barging into a conversation without waiting to be invited.

I wandered back upstairs and sat down on the edge of my bed, staring at the photo on the dresser of Mom holding me when I was two. I studied her face, her smile, trying my best to remember it. Lester says she was tall, she liked to sing, and she had the same color hair as I do. I'm not tall, I can't sing, so about the only thing we had in common was hair, and even that was changing.

And suddenly the sad feeling in my chest grew stronger until I felt panicky, as though maybe this wedding was a horrible mistake. After three years of desperately wanting Sylvia Summers for my stepmom, now I felt sad for my real mother.

Had Dad forgotten about her? When he kissed Sylvia, did he ever forget and murmur "Marie"? How could we be acting so happy when my real mother had died too young?

I jumped up suddenly and pulled the hall phone into my room. Then I dialed Pamela.

"What's up?" she said. She's got Caller ID and always knows it's me.

"P-P-Pamela . . . ," I wept. "Maybe it's all a mistake."

"Huh?" she said. "*What* is?"

"The w-wedding," I wailed.

"Have you lost your mind?"

"I can't stand it that maybe Dad's forgotten all about Mom," I croaked.

"How could he ever forget her when he's got you and Lester to remind him?" said Pamela. "What's the matter with you? Why are you talking like this all of a sudden?"

"I don't know. I'm worried that maybe Sylvia isn't the right woman for him."

"You *are* out of your mind. You've devoted the last three years of your life to getting them together, and now you've got the jitters. It's supposed to be the bride who gets the jitters, not the bridesmaid."

"But why hasn't she gotten married before?"

"*What?*"

"Why couldn't she get along better with her brother, and why did her sister get divorced? Maybe they're women who just use men and throw them away like Kleenex. Maybe they just—"

"I'm hanging up, Alice. Call me when you're sane."

"Maybe I should try to stop them before it's too late," I mewed. "Maybe when the minister says—"

I heard a click and then a dial tone. I bawled some more. Twenty seconds later the phone rang. I picked it up.

"You know who you sound like?" came Pamela's voice. "*Exactly* who you sound like? Elizabeth." And she hung up a second time.

That snapped me out of it in a hurry. If I didn't get hold of myself, I'd be worrying about Jim Sorringer following Dad and Sylvia on their honeymoon and trying to kidnap Sylvia and . . .

The honeymoon. Where *were* they going on their honeymoon? Were they even going anyplace at all?

Suddenly I was afraid that maybe they weren't! Maybe they were going to come right back here after the reception and spend their wedding night here! In this house! Only two rooms away from mine!

I called Pamela again.

"*Now* what?" she said.

"If they spend their honeymoon here, I'm coming over to your house for the duration," I said.

"Fine," said Pamela, and hung up for the third time.

After I washed my face and smeared some foundation on my nose, which was all red and shiny from crying, I went downstairs. Dad and Sylvia were sitting on the couch now, Sylvia's head on his shoulder.

"I never asked where you were going on your honeymoon," I said from the doorway. "Or is it secret?"

"It's not secret from you," Dad said, looking up and smiling. "We're driving to the Greenbrier Resort in West Virginia. We want to do some hiking and horseback riding . . . swimming. The leaves should be gorgeous the third week of October."

"Am I the only one who knows?"

"We haven't told anyone but you," said Sylvia.

Amazing how much better things look when you don't feel so left out. I thought of Amy Sheldon again—the way her face lit up when I told her she was invited to the wedding after all. I went back to my room, got out the percale sheets and pillowcases, and worked some more on the embroidery.

On Saturdays I have a job at my dad's music store, the Melody Inn. He's the manager, and an old girlfriend of Lester's, Marilyn Rawley, is assistant manager. I always hoped that she and Les would marry, but I guess that wasn't meant to be. She got tired of waiting for Lester to get serious about her, and now she's engaged to a guy named Jack.

"I'll bet things are really hopping at your place," she said when I came in that Saturday. "One more week and your dad will have himself a bride. I've never seen him so happy."

"Me either," I said, taking off my coat and going

behind the counter in the store's Gift Shoppe, where we sell musical gifts. There are two floors at the Melody Inn. Pianos, violins, and other musical instruments and sheet music on the first; instructors' cubicles for private lessons on the second. The Gift Shoppe is under the stairs; that's where I work.

"And to think you're the one who brought them together by inviting Sylvia to a Messiah Sing-Along," said Marilyn.

"All the more amazing when you consider that I can't even sing!" I said.

"Know what I'm giving them as a wedding present?" said Marilyn. "I had a copy of Handel's *Messiah* bound in leather, with 'Ben and Sylvia' and their wedding date stamped in gold letters on the cover."

"Oh, Marilyn, that's perfect!" I said, and wondered why I couldn't think of things like that.

"I thought it was pretty neat myself," she said, pleased that I thought so too.

I busied myself with restocking the shelves. Dad wasn't coming in at all that day, and Marilyn and I were trying to do as much of his work as we could. He had hired a new employee, a handsome guy of about eighteen named David. He was one of the greatest-looking guys I'd ever seen, with dark hair and a square jaw. He wore great-looking shirts too. On this particular morning he was wearing a dark blue shirt with a yellow tie. I wondered if he had a girlfriend.

"Hey!" he said when he saw me.

"Hey," I answered.

"You bring me anything good today?" he asked. I always bring a lunch on Saturdays, and he's been teasing me about bringing something for him too. But I forgot.

"Darn!" he said. "Guess it's up the street for chicken nuggets again."

Shortly after the store opened, a round-faced girl about my age came in and walked into the sheet music department. I glanced over to make sure that either Marilyn or David was there, and when I saw David wait on her, I went back to dusting shelves.

There was something about her, though, that made me look back—something familiar—and I was trying to decide if I'd seen her around school. I saw her pay for her purchase, and when she turned to leave, she caught me looking at her. She paused, started to walk out, then paused again. Finally she grinned and came over.

"Alice?" she said, hesitating.

I looked at her face, her cheeks, the funny familiar downward turn of her mouth at the corners. "*Rosalind?*" I said.

"Yes!"

"I don't *believe* it!" I cried, and suddenly we were hugging each other. One of my best friends in third, fourth, and fifth grades back in Takoma Park, and we hadn't seen each other in over four years. She had lost some weight, but she was still the roundest friend I had. On Rosalind, it looked good.

I gave her shoulders a shake. "How *are* you?"

"Same as always," she said. "How about you? Why didn't you ever call?"

"I went over to your house before we moved, but you'd gone on vacation without telling me. Why didn't *you* ever call?"

"I was never very good at good-byes," said Rosalind. She shrugged then and grinned. "*Fifth* graders! What can I say?"

I laughed. Then, thinking about the little band that our brothers had formed back in high school, I asked, "Remember the Naked Nomads?" That set us off, and we laughed some more.

"Does Lester still play the drums and the guitar?" she asked.

"He sold the drums. Sometimes I hear him playing the guitar, but he's in graduate school now, so he's pretty busy. What about Billy?"

"Bill? He still plays. In fact"—she held up the sack in her hand—"I just got him some guitar music for his birthday. He wants to go professional and plays in a band around town on weekends."

"Really? What about you? Are you ever going to get your dream job and work in a zoo?"

"I already do. I volunteer at the National Zoo."

"The elephant house?" I said, remembering how she'd talked about that back in grade school.

"How'd you guess?" she said. "The elephant house exactly."

"Listen, let's stay in touch this time," I told her. "I want to catch up on absolutely everything you've been doing since the end of fifth grade."

"Now that I know you're working here, I'll come back some Saturday and we can go somewhere for lunch," she said. Then, jiggling the sack again, she added, "I've got to get home and wrap this so at least *one* thing will go right for my brother today. His band is supposed to play for somebody's bar mitzvah next Saturday, and the bass player says he can't make it. Billy's got to find a substitute. It's the second time Sorringer's pulled this and—"

"Sorringer?" I said. "What's his first name?"

"Jim. You know him? He says he has to go to a wedding."

I think I could feel my stomach slide all the way down to my toes. I didn't know Jim Sorringer was musical. I didn't know he played bass. "He was vice principal of my junior high school, if we're talking about the same guy," I said, my head reeling with the news.

"That's him. He's a lot older than Bill, and I know he's a teacher or something. Between you and me, he's not a very good bass player, and Bill's going to find someone to replace him." Rosalind laughingly poked my arm. "But, hey, we're still in the phone book—same street, same number. Call me sometime."

"I'll call," I promised, and gave her a squeeze.

It was wonderful to see Rosalind again. I'd wondered from time to time how she was doing, but—being a typical kid—I had gotten busy with other things. Right at that minute, however, my mind was in turmoil. I had a terrible feeling that Jim Sorringer was planning to come to Dad and Sylvia's wedding, and I was 99 percent sure his name wasn't on the guest list.

3

The Relatives

I called Lester as soon as I got home, but the guy who answered told me he wasn't in.

"Who is this?" I asked.

"This is Paul, and who are *you*?" he asked. His voice was pleasant, though. Mine, I'm sure, was nearly hysterical.

"Alice," I said. "Would you ask Lester to call home as soon as possible?"

"Sure. Not an emergency, is it?"

"Not quite," I said.

It was an hour and a half before Lester called back. Dad was in the kitchen making supper, and as soon as I heard the phone ring, I ran upstairs and took it there.

"Al?" Lester said. "What's up?"

"Oh, Les, what are we going to do?" I asked. "Jim Sorringer is going to come to the wedding."

There was a long pause.

"Well?" I said. "What are we going to *do*?"

"Call in the National Guard?" said Lester.

"Lester, this is *serious*! You *know* he wasn't invited. He's only going to cause trouble."

"Okay," Lester said. "I'm going to conceal a six-inch Magnum inside my suit coat, and as soon as I see him walk through the door, I'll shoot him between the eyes. How's that?"

"Les-ter!"

"How do you *know* he's coming to cause trouble, Alice? Will you quit jumping to conclusions?"

"Should I tell Dad?"

"No, you shouldn't tell Dad! We are talking about mature, grown-up people here. And please quit leaving messages that give the impression the house burned down with everyone in it."

I hung up. For once I believed Lester was wrong. Mature, grown-up people don't buy an airline ticket to England, either, to visit a woman who is thinking about marrying somebody else, which is exactly what Mr. Sorringer did last Christmas. Sylvia didn't even know he was coming.

But I decided to keep my thoughts to myself for at least twenty-four hours and see if I still felt uneasy about it. It occurred to me, though, that maybe there were *two* Jim Sorringers, so on Sunday I called Elizabeth. "Do you happen to know if Jim Sorringer plays a musical instrument?" I asked.

"Hmm." She was thinking. "He played in a little band for one of our school talent shows," she said.

"Do you remember what instrument he played? I'm just curious," I told her.

"Bass, I think."

I swallowed. "Thanks, Liz," I said, and hung up.

By lunchtime on Monday, however, I was tired of being patient. There was a tragedy about to happen, and I was the only one who saw the danger. And so, seated between Liz and Pam at the table, I told them about seeing my old friend Rosalind at the Melody Inn and what she'd said about Jim Sorringer. It wasn't long before the whole table—both tables, in fact—knew that our assistant principal back in junior high was planning to come to Dad and Sylvia's wedding, invitation or not.

It was Penny who said the unthinkable, and now I *really* didn't like her: "How do you know he didn't get a personal invitation from Sylvia?"

I stared at her across the table, where she dangled a piece of lettuce between two fingers, then slowly stuffed it in her mouth.

"What do you mean by *that*?" I asked coldly. I still hadn't found out where she'd invited Patrick to go on the day of Dad's wedding and whether or not he'd accepted.

"I mean, maybe she just casually told Mr.

Sorringer he could come if he wanted. No biggie."
Penny looked even cuter and more petite than ever
as she sort of hunkered down inside her sweater.

"Sylvia would never do that!" Elizabeth volun-
teered.

"You don't even *know* Sylvia!" I told Penny,
excluding her all the more.

"Sorry. Just a thought to make you feel better,"
Penny said.

"How would that make me feel better?" I said, and
gave her a dismissive look. She finished her salad
and then moved over to the next table to talk to Jill.

Patrick came in then with his tray and took
Penny's chair. I told him what was up.

"So what do you think might happen if he
comes?" he asked.

"I'm not sure," I said. "All I know is that he does
impulsive things, so anything could happen."

Brian, who's as large as a linebacker, pushed his
hamburger to one side of his mouth and said,
"You want us to deck him if he shows?"

"What?"

"Act as bouncers. Usher him out."

"You actually would?"

"Just give the word," said Mark, and Patrick
nodded.

"We're not in junior high anymore," he said,
and jokingly flexed one arm.

I think he was serious, though. I think all the guys were serious. In fact, I think every boy who ever had Sylvia Summers for a teacher was halfway in love with her.

"Well, when you come to the wedding, why don't you just sit near the door, and if he comes in, go stand next to him. Don't 'bounce' him if he's not doing anything," I told them.

"Gotcha," said Brian.

"We won't start anything. He'll have to make the first move," said Patrick.

"You're coming, then?" I asked Patrick. "To the wedding?"

"Well, of course. You invited me, didn't you?" he said, and I wanted to cast a triumphant look in Penny's direction, but I restrained myself.

"You guys are great," I told them. Dad and Sylvia had absolutely no idea how much work I had put into keeping them together.

At the lockers, though, after lunch, we were talking about what the guys had said, and Pamela said, "When you think about it, Alice, if you were Jim Sorringer's daughter . . ."

"What do you mean?" I asked.

"Well, your dad *did* steal her away from him; so if it were the other way around . . ."

I felt myself bristle. Not Pamela, too! "Well, it's not like he kidnapped her or anything," I said. "I invited her to the Messiah Sing-Along, and she discovered she and Dad had a lot in common, that's all."

"Yeah, just like Mom and her aerobics instructor," Pamela said.

That was about the worst thing Pamela had ever said to me. I wheeled around. "Pamela!" I said. Pamela's mom had run off with the guy who was showing her how to use the NordicTrack. Dad and Sylvia hadn't done anything at all like that!

"I'm just making a point," Pamela said. "I mean, you can't exactly hold it against Jim Sorringer for wanting her back, can you?"

I supposed not. All through English that afternoon I sat scribbling on the back of my notebook. I wasn't even aware of what I was doing until I saw whole columns and rows of delicate *SSM* monograms for *Sylvia Summers McKinley* alternating with rows of *SSS* monograms for *Sylvia Summers Sorringer.* I realized with a pang that I had only a few more nights to finish embroidering the sheets and pillowcases I was giving Dad and Sylvia as a wedding present, and I got that panicky feeling again.

But it wasn't just the sheets and pillowcases that did it. It was the fact that Sylvia wasn't the first woman Dad had lured away from another man.

Aunt Sally told me once that before Dad knew Mom, she had been engaged to a man named Charlie Snow. But after Dad met her, he decided she was the woman for him and wrote her such beautiful love letters that she gave back Charlie's ring and married Dad instead. I wished Mom were still alive so I could ask her about that. About Charlie Snow . . . love . . . life . . .

On the bus going home that afternoon, I squeezed in between Pamela and Elizabeth.

"What's the matter with *her*?" Elizabeth said to Pamela as I felt a tear roll down my cheek.

"Pre-wedding jitters," said Pamela. "If she's like this as a bridesmaid, can you imagine what she'll be like as a bride? The other day she was worried that Sylvia was the kind of woman who discards a man like Kleenex." They both looked at me pityingly. "So what is it *now*?"

"What if . . . what if my dad's a home-wrecker?" I said in a barely audible voice.

"A *what*?"

"What if he's only attracted to women who are loved by another man?" I sounded so much like Elizabeth, I was embarrassed to be saying it in front of her.

But it was Elizabeth, surprisingly, who said the wisest words of the afternoon: "If your dad was a home-wrecker, Alice, he's had ten years since your mom died to wreck a couple of marriages and then some. Instead, he's been waiting all this time for just the right woman to come along, and now she's here."

I laid my head on Elizabeth's shoulder. Not even Aunt Sally could have said it better.

That evening Martin Small, one of the instructors at the Melody Inn, came over with another of the musicians who were going to play at the wedding—the cellist. The violinist was late, and Dad said he'd play that part until she came. I said hi and went up to my room to work on my embroidery while they practiced.

I never like to be in the same room with musicians. I'd rather listen to them than watch, because I focus on their faces instead of the music. Some musicians rock back and forth when they play, and some wrinkle up their foreheads. When I was small, I remember Dad taking me to a concert. The piano player leaned so far back, I thought he was going to fall off the piano bench, and I laughed out loud. So I usually go up to my room when there's a music session going on.

But this time, as my needle went in and out of the percale, I listened hard. I imagined the ensemble up front at the church, playing as the guests came in and were seated. Dad had already talked about liking the third movement of the trio best, so I knew there would be three movements with pauses between them. When the third one began, it would be my cue that the wedding march was only minutes away.

The first movement reminded me of the way Dad was when Sylvia fell in love with him: happy. *Perfect,* I thought. *Happy music for a happy day.* But when the second movement began, slower and somber, I felt that panicky feeling again. I remembered Dad's face when he found out that Jim Sorringer had flown to England to surprise Sylvia at Christmas. I remembered the way he had puttered aimlessly around the house last summer when Nancy got sick and the wedding had to be postponed.

This is the way it will always be, I reminded myself. *The way life will always be—happy and sad and scary and exciting and never knowing what will happen next.* And, as if to prove it, when the third movement began, there was the excitement, the happiness again, with just a few sad notes mixed in.

They hadn't quite reached the end when the doorbell rang and the violinist arrived. When the musicians played the piece for the second time, I was ready for it—the sad parts, too. I knew they would be over soon and the music would be joyful again. And so would I.

4

The Jitters

What I wanted, this week of the wedding, was for time to stand still so I could concentrate on what had to be done. But teachers went right on giving assignments as though the most wonderful wedding in the world weren't taking place on Saturday. And it wasn't just the teachers. I'm the sophomore roving reporter for our school newspaper, *The Edge,* and I even got an assignment from our new editor, a tall dark-haired senior named Jayne Renaldi.

"You know that class Mrs. Frazier is teaching this year, Practical Living?" she said at the staff meeting. "Things all seniors should know before they graduate?"

"You mean the one where you learn to balance a checkbook and change a lightbulb?" someone asked, and we laughed.

"That's the one. I thought it might be fun if we

surveyed a sample of students ourselves and asked them what practical thing *they* would like to learn before they graduate. Make our own list and publish it in the paper."

We thought it was a pretty good idea.

"When's the deadline?" someone asked.

"Make it October twentieth, next Monday," said Jayne.

Oh, wow! I thought. Two days after the wedding. Why does everything have to pile up at once? *Life's rough,* Lester would say if I complained to him.

But in addition to my schoolwork, this wasn't just the last week to finish embroidering a present; it was also the week the relatives would arrive. Dad was half crazy with stuff he had to do. He only went to the Melody Inn a few hours each day. I decided I'd better call Sylvia and see if there was anything I could do for her, because she didn't have a nearby family member to help out at all.

I waited until I figured she'd be home from school on Wednesday, then dialed her number. The phone rang five times before she answered, and she sounded rushed.

"I just wondered if there was anything I could do to help," I said. "Dad's going a little bit nuts here with all he has to do, so I was worrying about you."

She laughed. "Oh, you're sweet, but actually, I

was just heading out the door when you called. My girlfriends are giving me a 'Girls Night Out' party, so I've got to run."

"Oh!" I said in surprise. Then, "Oh!" again. "Well, have fun!" I said, and hung up.

I didn't take my hand off the phone. Was this what I thought it was? A bachelorette party? I lifted the phone again and called Lester. Miraculously, he was home.

"I just want to know, Les. Are you giving Dad a bachelor party?" I asked.

"Are you crazy?" he answered. "As though we don't have enough to do?"

The phone hadn't been put down again five seconds when it rang. It was Elizabeth. "Pamela's here, and we're trying to decide what to wear to the wedding," she said. "Want to come over?"

I did. They had five outfits draped across one of Elizabeth's twin beds, and were trying out different jackets and jewelry to see which went with what. I sat down in a chair in the corner and gave a thumbs-up or thumbs-down to each new combination they showed me. Elizabeth decided on a blue dress with an ivory chemise, while Pamela chose a black strappy dress that showed off her shoulders. This settled, we poured ourselves some Mountain Dew, and Elizabeth and Pamela sprawled on the other bed.

"You know where Sylvia is right this minute?" I said.

"Where?" they asked.

"A bachelorette party."

Pamela gave a whistle. "Her last night to howl," she said. "Love those Chippendales!"

"She wouldn't," said Elizabeth. "She wouldn't go watch nude men prancing around, would she, Alice?"

"I'll bet she even goes up and slips a twenty in a G-string." Pamela giggled.

Elizabeth kept her eyes on me, waiting. It was as though if I said yes, Sylvia would do something like that, then all of Western civilization would crumble.

"I don't know," I said truthfully. "Maybe they're just all at a ritzy bar somewhere, having a couple drinks and telling each other intimate secrets."

"That's almost worse," said Elizabeth.

I propped my feet on the bed beside Elizabeth and Pamela. "How is that worse?"

"Because if you're talking about how far you went with a guy, it won't belong to you and your boyfriend anymore. It's out in the open, where anyone can grab hold of it."

Pamela and I exchanged glances.

"Grab hold of *what*?" Pamela said. "You told us about Ross kissing your breasts at camp, and none of us grabbed hold of them." We grinned. It is *so* easy to get Liz worked up.

Elizabeth's face flushed. "And I never should have told you, because now it's not private anymore. I've wished a hundred times that I'd never told you guys that night, because that should belong to Ross and me and nobody else."

I leaned my head back in the chair. "Okay, I am going to hypnotize myself into forgetting that you ever told us," I said, and slowly dangled my house key back and forth in front of my face.

"Me too," said Pamela, turning over on her back. She fished inside her bag, looking for something of hers to dangle, and finally pulled out a tampon. Pushing it out of its applicator, she held it by its string, and we struggled to keep from laughing. "What do we do now?" she asked me.

Back and forth went the key in front of me. "I see a girl and a guy . . . walking through the woods . . . ," I began, trancelike.

"Holding hands . . . ," said Pamela softly.

"Now . . . they're stopping . . . and gently . . . he . . . kisses her on the mouth . . . and they . . . move on," I said.

"But wait!" said Pamela, swinging the tampon above her face like a dead mouse. "They stumble! They fall!" The tampon began to swing faster. "He falls *over* her . . . *on* her! They're moving up to the starting gate, and then . . . they're off! Elizabeth on the inside, Ross on the outside, Ross moving up, Elizabeth against the rail . . ."

"Oh, you guys!" Liz laughed.

"Elizabeth in the lead! Ross gaining!" The tampon was going like crazy. "He's on the sweatshirt! He's *under* her sweatshirt! And it's . . . Ross! Ross by a nose and a tongue. Ross wins the Triple Crown! Yahoo!"

We were all laughing now, and Elizabeth's little brother peeked in the room to see what was going on.

"See? I've forgotten already, Elizabeth!" I said. "I know it had something to do with lips and leaves and sweatshirts, but I haven't the foggiest idea what we were talking about."

"Well, *I* do! It's about Ross kissing her naked breasts, and this is implanted in my brain forever!" said Pamela.

"I'll never tell you guys another thing!" Elizabeth said, playfully giving us each a kick.

"Until Ross comes to visit," Pamela said. "Then we'll hear all about it. You *know* you're going to tell!"

I found out later from Dad what Sylvia did on Girls Night Out, and as soon as I got on the bus the next morning, I squeezed into a seat between Elizabeth and Pamela.

"I got the whole story," I whispered mysteriously, "but you have to promise you'll never tell a living soul or it could be the end of their marriage."

Elizabeth sucked in her breath. *"What?"* she whispered.

"Well, Sylvia and her girlfriends went to this private place . . ." I lowered my eyes. "And . . . one at a time . . . they each took off their clothes."

Pamela stared at me.

"Everything?" Elizabeth asked. "Even their underpants?"

"Everything!" I said. "And then . . . one at a time . . . they each lay down, and this man came in . . ."

"And *what*?" Elizabeth gasped, her eyes huge.

"And gave them a massage," I finished, and burst out laughing.

They laughed too, and Elizabeth looked decidedly relieved.

"They gave Sylvia a private party at the Red Door Salon and Spa. They all got massages, facials, manicures, pedicures—the works. And then they all went out to dinner."

"I *knew* she wouldn't do anything awful," said Elizabeth. "I *knew* she'd be true to your dad." But then she looked thoughtful. "Do you have to get naked to have a massage?"

"Well, you've got a sheet over your privates," said Pamela. "He only uncovers a little bit at a time."

"Does it have to be a he?"

"Doesn't have to," I told her, "but it sure makes it a lot more exciting." As though I knew anything about it!

That evening—Thursday—I rode to the airport with Lester to pick up Aunt Sally, Uncle Milt, and their daughter, Carol. Dad had reserved two rooms for them at the Holiday Inn in Silver Spring, where we live. But the minute Les told them about his bachelor apartment, Carol said, "Oh, Les, let me stay with you!"

I was sitting in the backseat between my aunt and uncle and heard Les say, "Sure! We'd love to have you!"

I think Aunt Sally stopped breathing. Uncle Milt's getting hard of hearing, so it went right over his head. He was looking out the window, watching a huge crane at a construction site, but Lester's answer was like a huge crane itself, taking up all the space in the car.

"Carol!" said her mother. "You can't just invite yourself over to a man's apartment like that! Where would you sleep?"

"She can have my bed," said Lester. "I'll take the

couch." Then he added mischievously, "Unless she'd prefer to bunk with George or Paul."

Carol and I laughed, but Aunt Sally drew in a long breath. One of the problems of growing old, I think, is how much harder it must be to know when people are teasing. Did Aunt Sally really believe that Carol would walk into Lester's apartment, look the guys over, and go, *Eenie, meenie, minie, mo?*

I stole a look at Aunt Sally, the way her face had tensed up. *Yep,* I thought. *She does.*

Lester says that Aunt Sally and our mom were very different, even though they were sisters. Aunt Sally's hair is gray now, but it used to be strawberry blond like Mom's. Only Mom wore hers loose about her face, while Aunt Sally keeps hers permed in tight little curls around her scalp. Her head always reminds me of a cabbage.

She was four years older than Mom, always too grown-up for her age, I've heard, while Mom was the free spirit, sort of like Carol. Lester says if we'd been born to Aunt Sally, he probably would have grown up to be a bookkeeper and I'd be in a convent, and we're not even Catholic. But how do we explain Carol? Pretty, vivacious, funny, and divorced. That's Carol.

"That's settled, then!" Lester said brightly. "And we just saved you the price of a room. You're going to love our place. We decided to knock out a whole wall between an old sitting room and a bedroom. Makes a great living room/kitchen combination with stove, sink, and fridge in a closet."

"Sounds terrific!" said Carol.

But to Aunt Sally, I suppose, it sounded like trouble.

Sylvia's sister had come in that afternoon at Dulles Airport, and Lois—Sylvia's college roommate—had driven up from North Carolina. The three of them were going to have a quiet dinner together at Sylvia's to give Nancy a chance to rest. So Uncle Milt and Aunt Sally took Dad to dinner. I begged off in order to finish my homework assignments—I knew I wouldn't have any time over the weekend. What I really needed to do was work on embroidering that sheet and pillowcase set. The rehearsal dinner was the following night, the wedding the day after that . . .

I set to work on one of the flowers and managed to call a few kids while I was at it and ask what practical thing they would like to learn before they graduated.

"Put on eyeliner," said Jill.

"Fake an ID," said Brian.

When I heard Dad come in, I hurriedly put all the thread away, along with the sheets, and managed to have my biology book out when he came upstairs.

"Still at it?" he said, stopping by my room.

"Yeah," I told him. "How was dinner? Has Aunt Sally recovered from shock?"

Dad just chuckled. "She'll always be Sally," he said. "I imagine I'll even sound like her in a few years."

"Tell me something," I said. "Why do adults assume that all you have to do is put a guy and girl alone together and immediately aliens take over their brains and the next thing you know they're in bed?"

"Because sometimes it happens, even without aliens," Dad said.

"Les is twenty-three now," I said, "and Carol's even older."

"I know," said Dad.

"Carol's divorced and Lester's had a few relationships. It's not like they haven't been around."

"I know," said Dad.

"So when is Aunt Sally going to stop worrying about her?"

"Never." Dad smiled. "She's a mother, Al. It goes with the territory."

We got through the rehearsal on Friday without any major goofs. But Nancy decided she just didn't feel well enough to stand on her feet during the whole ceremony, so I would be maid of honor. Lester was best man; Kirk—Sylvia's brother—would walk her down the aisle; and Uncle Harold and Uncle Howard, Dad's brothers from Tennessee, would serve as ushers. Except that they hadn't arrived yet, so we had the rehearsal without them. Nancy sat in one of the pews and watched.

"Hello, Alice," she said when we met, and she smiled the same kind of warm smile that Sylvia did. Her eyes were gray, not blue, and she looked a bit puffy around the face, but I think I could have guessed she was Sylvia's sister.

"I'm glad you're better," I said.

"So am I. And I know you're going to be a fine maid of honor in my place," she said.

I was curious about Sylvia's brother, though— about Kirk and his whole family, in fact. He was tall—taller than Dad—and his hair was gray around the temples. He had a square face with a wide forehead, and his wife looked a lot like him. It's strange sometimes the way a husband and wife start looking like each other. They had a son, I'd heard, who was in the Marine Corps, but their nineteen-year-old daughter—Margaret— had come, and she and her mom sat in the pew with Nancy during the rehearsal.

What was it about Kirk that was so different from Sylvia? I wondered. He and his wife and even Margaret seemed so uptight, as though things had to be done exactly right or it wouldn't be a proper wedding. Just the way they sat, the way they smiled or didn't smile. The formal-sounding way they talked.

"How do you do, Alice?" Kirk had said to me after he'd been introduced to Dad. Then his wife asked, "How do you do?" and Margaret said, "How do you do?" and I wondered if I should just go down the row and answer, "Fine . . . fine . . . fine." But he had flown out here for Sylvia, and I was determined to be nice to everybody, even Margaret when she took me aside without my asking and instructed me on how to walk down the aisle.

Step . . . pause . . . step . . . pause. Margaret told me to memorize the exact spot where I should stand after I walked down the aisle ahead of Sylvia and to line myself up with a certain window on the other side of the sanctuary.

"As soon as Sylvia reaches the altar," Margaret said, "she'll hand you her bouquet. But in case she forgets, you need to reach out and take it from her."

Step . . . pause . . . step . . . pause. . . . Don't forget to smile. . . . Lift each foot so you don't trip on your dress. . . . Take the bouquet. . . . The more rules

Margaret gave me, the more nervous I became.

I was glad when we were done at last, and we set off for the rehearsal dinner. Uncle Harold called and said that they had been delayed and that they'd decided to go right to the hotel and get Grandpa settled. And that's where the dinner would be held.

We pulled into the hotel parking lot and helped Nancy up the steps to the lobby, then on into the private dining room Dad had reserved for us.

I'll bet Queen Elizabeth wouldn't have attracted more attention than Sylvia when she walked in that room, and Sylvia wasn't even trying. She was wearing a green and gold dress, the two colors sort of melting into each other in flares about the skirt. She smiled at everyone in the room as Dad led her toward the Tennessee contingent of McKinleys on one side.

Grandpa McKinley was sitting in his wheelchair, all spiffed up in a white shirt and freshly pressed trousers. His fingers were curled over the arms of the chair, and he looked confused at all the activity. I was waiting to hug my uncles and their wives, but Dad had got there first so I was left facing Grandpa.

"Hi, Grandpa," I said, stepping forward and kissing him on the cheek.

He brightened and looked up at me. "Marie?" he said, seeming surprised.

I was startled. Did I really look that much like my mom? I wondered.

"No, I'm Alice. I'm her daughter," I said. "Ben and Marie's daughter." He gets confused a lot. He looked at me hard, but then Dad and Sylvia came over.

Dad leaned down and hugged him, then let Grandpa study his face. "I'm so glad you could come, Dad," he said.

"Durn long way up here. Hard on the legs," Grandpa rasped.

"I know, but it wouldn't have been complete without you. Now I want you to meet Sylvia."

Sylvia knelt down so that Grandpa could see her face, and she took his hands in hers. "Hello, Mr. McKinley," she said. "I've wanted to meet you for a long time."

"Why's that?" he asked.

"Because I've always wanted to meet the father of the man I'm going to marry," Sylvia told him.

"You're going to marry Ben?"

"Yes." Sylvia fixed her blue eyes on him. We all held our breath. You just never know what Grandpa McKinley is going to say next.

"Well, we'll just see what Marie has to say about that!" was what he said.

Everybody stopped talking and smiling and stared at Grandpa, then at Dad to see what he would do.

Dad put his hand on Grandpa's shoulder. "Dad, Marie died ten years ago. Do you remember?"

"Why, that's terrible!" said Grandpa, his face collapsing. His hands slipped off the arms of the wheelchair and lay helplessly in his lap. "Gladys and Marie and Charlie, all gone," he said, remembering not only his wife and daughter-in-law, but his son Charlie, who had died a few years back. He seemed small and shrunken in his wheelchair.

Sylvia didn't even blink. "Ben told me that his mother was a beautiful woman," she said.

Grandpa began to smile.

"And I'll bet you made a handsome couple on *your* wedding day," she went on.

Grandpa leaned forward, and his eyes took on a mischievous look. "I was something of a dandy," he whispered loudly. "They used to call me 'the cat's pajamas'!"

We all laughed then, and Grandpa laughed with us.

But there were aunts and uncles yet to introduce, as well as Sylvia's sister. I saw Sylvia's brother come in with his wife and Margaret, and then Aunt Sally and Uncle Milt, with Carol. Aunt Sally had not even met the woman who was taking my mom's place.

Carol and her dad were no problem. Carol greeted Sylvia and her sister as though they were long-lost sisters themselves, and Uncle Milt likes everybody. It was Aunt Sally who was having a hard time with the idea of Dad marrying again, I could tell.

And how could she not? How could she welcome Dad's new wife-to-be without thinking of her sister? Without remembering Mom and Dad's wedding day and how she'd been the maid of honor that time? I saw her pause as she turned around and saw Sylvia. Noticed the way she swallowed when she saw Dad's arm around Sylvia's waist. But when Dad introduced them, Aunt Sally grasped Sylvia's arms and studied her face. Then she said, "Ten years is a long time to grieve for someone, Sylvia. I'm Marie's sister, and I'm glad that Ben has you."

I had promised to call Elizabeth and Pamela as soon as I got home and tell them all about the rehearsal dinner, but Pamela was out, so I just talked to Elizabeth.

"I feel so ignorant!" I said. "I have no idea what my other duties are as maid of honor, and I wasn't about to ask Margaret! She's given me enough rules already."

"Oh, Alice," she said. "That's about the most important job there is! My aunt was a maid of honor last summer, and it took her a year to do all she was supposed to do."

"The wedding's *tomorrow,* Elizabeth."

"That means you don't have to give her a shower or anything, but I know for a fact that you're supposed to be prepared for anything that might happen."

When did Elizabeth start sounding like Miss Manners? I wondered.

"Well, we've already got a contingency plan in case Jim Sorringer shows up," I said. "What else am I supposed to do?"

"Your three biggest jobs are to hold her bouquet during the ceremony, pull back her veil so your dad can kiss her, and readjust her train when they turn to leave."

I tried to program them into my brain. *Bouquet,* I said to myself. Yes, we'd rehearsed that part. *Pull back veil. Adjust train.*

"I think she decided not to have the veil over her face, and she told me that her dress doesn't have a train," I said, remembering.

"Okay, then, but you're supposed to carry every single thing Sylvia could possibly need for the entire day," said Elizabeth.

"Like what?" I asked, and envisioned myself coming down the aisle with a suitcase.

"Tampons," said Elizabeth.

"She's had a hysterectomy!" I reminded her.

"Oh. Right. Well, you should have Kleenex,

then. Lipstick, powder, safety pins, comb, barf bag—"

"What?" I said.

"It happens! My aunt heard of a bride who was so tired and nervous that when she got up to the altar, she puked all over the groom and the preacher."

"Elizabeth!"

"I'm just telling you this for your own good."

I remembered how Sylvia had thrown up when she got off the plane coming back from England. It could happen!

I was nervous enough thinking about holding the two bouquets. Now I was supposed to hold my bouquet, Sylvia's bouquet, a purse filled with things for Sylvia, plus a full barf bag?

"And *then* what would I do with it—the barf bag?" I asked incredulously.

"Take it back up the aisle with you! You certainly don't hand it to the minister!" said Elizabeth.

"Yeah, right," I said. "Well, I've got to go."

I hung up the phone and sat with my hand on it. Nancy had been all prepared to be Sylvia's maid of honor. If anyone should know what my responsibilities were, she would. I dialed Sylvia's number. Sylvia answered.

"Well, hello, Alice," she said.

"I was wondering if I could talk to Nancy."

"Oh, she was really tired and went right to bed when we got home," she said. There was a pause. "Can I help?"

I knew I wasn't supposed to talk to Sylvia about this. You should never get a bride nervous the day before the wedding. "I . . . I just wanted to say how nice it was to meet her," I said lamely.

"I'm sure she feels the same way about you," Sylvia said.

"Well," I said awkwardly. "Have a nice night."

"You too, Alice," she said. "We've got a big day ahead of us."

I hung up the phone and rested my forehead on my knees. *Oh, please,* I thought, *just let us get through tomorrow without any problems. Let Dad marry Sylvia and Sylvia not throw up and me not trip on my long dress and* especially . . . *don't let Jim Sorringer ruin the whole thing.*

5

Yes!

When I woke up Saturday morning, I took a look around my bedroom. Everything was about to change, I thought. Then I reminded myself that my room wouldn't change.

My jungle bedspread was still here, my tropical plant, my old fur-and-plastic monkey I rediscovered in the attic. No matter how Dad and Sylvia might change the rest of the house, this room would be mine forever, my own little space, my hideaway.

I stared at the light that slipped in above my curtains. Not forever. Two and a half years more before college, maybe. Six and a half years if I went to a local college and lived at home. At what age could parents kick you out? I wondered.

Hey! What am I doing in bed? I asked myself. This was it! This was the day I'd been waiting for ever since I saw Miss Summers in seventh grade!

I threw off my blanket and hurried across the hall to the bathroom. As I brushed my teeth I realized this might be my last breakfast alone with Dad. Maybe he had fixed pecan pancakes for just the two of us. I put on my robe and started down the stairs.

Dad was on the phone in the hall, going over last-minute details with the photographer. I wandered out to the kitchen. There wasn't any breakfast waiting at all—just half a pot of coffee warming on the stove. I dawdled so Dad could finish his conversation, but when he hung up, he dialed Lester to see if someone was in charge of bringing back any gifts that were brought to the reception. I reached for the cornflakes and ate a solitary breakfast, then went upstairs and took my shower.

I was heading back to my room in my terry-cloth robe, a towel around my head, when the phone rang. I answered in the upstairs hall.

"Is this Alice?" asked a woman's voice.

"Yes . . ."

"I'm Lois, Sylvia's roommate from college. I'm on my way over to pick you up. Sylvia's instructions."

"Now?" I said, still dripping water on the rug. "I'm not dressed! I'm not even dry!"

"Perfect!" said Lois. "Just bring your dress and

shoes and undies, and come out to the car in your robe. We'll take care of the rest."

I giggled. "Okay!" I said, and flew into action. I had barely stuffed my underwear and shoes in a shopping bag when the phone rang again.

"It's Lois," came the voice. "I'm on a cell phone, actually, and I'm right outside your house. I've been running errands all morning."

I put on some sandals and clattered downstairs, the towel still around my head, bag in one hand, dress in the other.

"Al?" said Dad, staring.

"See you at the church, Dad!" I said gaily, and pushed open the screen door

Elizabeth was on the driveway across the street, picking up the newspaper.

"Alice!" she cried when she saw me, and I waved, laughing. I struck a pose, my arms outstretched, one foot forward, and suddenly my robe parted in front. Elizabeth and I shrieked together as I yanked it shut.

Lois was laughing too as she leaned over and opened the passenger-side door. "Better get in before you get arrested," she said, and helped me spread out my gown on the backseat. She was blond, with close-cropped hair, like Pamela's, and magnificent cheekbones. Her legs were long, and I imagined that she and Sylvia must have been pretty popular together in college.

"Big day, huh?" she said. "I haven't seen Sylvia this excited since we went on our first double date together."

"I feel utterly, completely naked," I said, pulling my robe together over my bare legs.

"Well, you are!" she said with a laugh. "But we'll fix that in a hurry. We've got a crew all ready to make you over."

"A *crew*? I'm such a wreck, it takes a *crew*?"

She grinned. "Well, Sylvia's sister-in-law and niece. Don't worry. I won't let them do anything drastic." And twenty minutes later we pulled up in front of Sylvia's little house in Kensington.

I felt as though I were on an assembly line. I was perfumed, deodorized, powdered, moussed, blow-dried, arranged, and sprayed. And that was just my hair and body. Back in the bedroom some of Sylvia's teacher friends were working on her.

After putting on my gown, I was ushered to the dining-room table, where Margaret waited to do my face. There was a mirror propped against a stack of books, and I never saw so many cosmetics spread out in front of me. Maybe it was a good thing that Margaret was a perfectionist; I wouldn't want somebody making my eyebrows uneven or putting the lip gloss on crooked.

First a moisturizer on my face and neck. Then foundation liquid makeup, the color of my skin, rouge on my cheekbones, and loose powder patted over my entire face. I'll have to admit, Margaret must have had a lot of practice, because everything she did looked good. Her mother stood by to do the final touching up.

Sylvia's sister was lying on the couch resting, and she smiled at me as she watched me being transformed. The royal blue gown she was supposed to wear in the bridal party lay draped over the back of a chair.

"I'm sorry you're not going to be in the ceremony, Nancy," I said.

"I'm disappointed I'm not feeling strong enough to get through it on my feet, Alice, but I'm having a good time watching you," she said. "And I'm going to go right ahead and wear the dress anyway."

"Good for you," I told her.

"Now hold completely still," said Margaret. "Don't blink, and don't even breathe if you can help it." I did my best, and she carefully began applying eyeliner to my lower and upper lids, as close to the lashes as she could possibly get on top and close to the inner rim of the lower lid, making little dots instead of a long straight line. I could see what she was doing in the mirror, and I noticed that she was putting the liner on only the outer two thirds of both lids. "Makes your eyes look wider apart," she explained. Then she carefully smudged the liner, added eye shadow, mascara on my lashes, and she gently brushed my eyebrows.

Next my nails.

I kept stealing looks at myself in the mirror. It was still me, but my good features were more pronounced. For some reason my eyes looked even more green, the strawberry highlights in my hair more red. I suddenly realized that I had cheekbones too. I just hadn't emphasized them before.

"Wow!" I said, to no one in particular. "I'm gorgeous!"

The women laughed, but behind me I heard someone say, "Of course you are. You're even gorgeous without all that stuff."

And there was Sylvia, in a long white satin gown. It was a simple sleeveless design, with a lace panel down the front. There were slits on either side of the skirt, giving a glimpse of her sling-back white satin shoes.

"Oh, Sylvia!" I breathed. "It's a fairy-tale dress!"

She smiled. "It's a fairy-tale day," she told me. Her nail polish was the color of mine, Rusty Rose, and she wore her hair up, showing off her beautiful neck in back. The veil was gathered away from her face, held in place by the floating pearl headband. Breathlessly beautiful was the way I'd describe her.

Here I was, the maid of honor, but I couldn't think of one single thing I'd done to help Sylvia get ready. When I told her that, though, she just laughed and said, "Well, you brought your dad and me together. I'd say that was a lot, wouldn't you?"

We all helped Nancy into her dress and did her hair before Kirk came by to pick her up. With people actually leaving for the church, I could feel the excitement building inside me. I glanced at the clock, then at Sylvia. Only a little while longer and she would be my stepmom.

At ten thirty a white stretch limousine pulled up in front. Carrying her bouquet, I helped Sylvia down the steps as neighbors watched from their porches, waving and smiling, and—once inside the limo—I carefully gathered her veil and placed it around her shoulders so it wouldn't wrinkle.

Everything seemed so surreal. I'd never been in a limo before. Sylvia sat at the very back, Lois and I on the side seats facing in, and Margaret and her mother on the seat behind the driver, facing us. The long white car rolled noiselessly down the street and around the corner, not far from the church on Cedar Lane.

"I didn't know you could see so well out the windows. They always looked dark to me," I said.

"We can see out, but nobody can see in," Lois explained. "So if we wanted, we could all get up on our hands and knees and moon the world."

I giggled and Sylvia grinned. "Leave it to Lois!" she said. "The craziest roommate I ever had." Margaret and her mother gave us anemic little smiles, and that almost made me burst out laughing, but I checked myself.

You wouldn't even know there was a church down in those trees if it weren't for the sign at the driveway entrance. It just looks like a deep woods, but there it was, with high glass walls on either side of the sanctuary, made up of several hundred little glass panels, and nothing to see through them but the October leaves.

I backed out of the limo first, giving my hand to Sylvia.

"Yay!" came a chorus from behind me when Sylvia stepped out, and there were Elizabeth and Pamela and Gwen and Lori, waiting for us.

"You go, girl!" called Gwen, and we all laughed.

A special room in the church was called the Bride's Room, and Sylvia did her last-minute adjusting there while the guests were coming in. I was relieved to see that she had her own little bag with her, which we would carry to the reception for her, but I had brought a small ivory-colored clutch to hold under my arm with some safety pins in it, one of Dad's large handkerchiefs, and just to be on the safe side, a waxed bag from Krispy Kreme doughnuts to use as a barf bag at the altar, just in case Sylvia got sick.

Standing there in the Bride's Room, listening to the start of the music, I remembered what Aunt Sally had said before, about ten years being a long time to grieve. I wished Dad had met Sylvia earlier—that he could have had *more* years of being her husband. But then, of course, Dad and Les and I wouldn't have had all these years of being so close. I didn't know what I wished except that we would get through this wedding without anything awful happening.

While Lois fussed with Sylvia's dress and hair, it was my job to stand at the door and listen for the end of Martin Small's composition and the start of the wedding march. I was pleased that I could recognize the three instruments—the violin playing the melody, the piano, and the cello adding its mellow accompaniment. And this time the parts that had made me feel sad before didn't bother me at all, and I smiled when the second movement was over and the third began.

I peeked into the sanctuary. Not only were all the seats filled, but so were most of the extra chairs that had been set up near the back. There are doors at the end of our sanctuary, and when there's a really big crowd, we can open those doors and put chairs all the way out into the foyer. I saw so many students that I began to think there wouldn't be room for any grown-up guests. Uncle Harold and Uncle Howard were performing their job as ushers, even though they hadn't made it to the rehearsal. I guess by the time you reach your sixties, you've been an usher at so many weddings that you know the ropes backward and forward.

Everyone was listening to the music, though, and it was fast and happy again, one note tumbling over another, like everything was sliding into place, right up to those final, finishing notes. And here it was, their wedding day! That was our cue.

In the hush that followed the end of the third movement, I sensed that the listeners almost wanted to applaud but knew they shouldn't. There was a soft rustling sound as the musicians put one piece of music aside and took out another. All the guests sat up a little straighter, and some of them looked around. I ducked back into the Bride's Room.

"We're about ready, Sylvia!" I said.

She smiled and took a deep breath, held it, then let it out.

"Let the wild rumpus begin!" said Lois, and we moved out into the hall. A small bead of perspiration slid down between my breasts and nestled between the lace cups of my Victoria's Secret bra. One of the spaghetti straps on my long teal dress was looser than the other, but it was in no danger of falling off my shoulder. I knew I looked good, and I just wanted to get moving. I knew I wouldn't feel so nervous once my body was actually *doing* something.

The ensemble began the familiar, joyful wedding march.

"This is it, baby!" I heard Lois say.

Holding my bouquet in front of me, my little silk clutch hidden beneath my arm, I took my first step down the aisle. The ribbons at the end of each row of seats were a cluster of teal, ivory, and royal blue, and I thought how perfect it would have been if Nancy had been in the procession in her royal blue dress to go with my gown of teal.

Dad and Lester were waiting at the altar, handsome in their dark blue suits—Lester in a red-and-blue tie, Dad in a blue-and-silver one. I realized I hadn't seen Lester all morning, and Dad had still been wearing an old sweatshirt when I left the house. But now there was something about Dad's face that made him look ten years younger. Everything about him was smiling—his eyes, his cheeks, his mouth—I'd swear, even his ears were smiling.

Step . . . pause . . . step . . . pause. . . . Lord, please don't let me stumble. I breathed deeply. *Step . . . pause . . .*

I smiled, too, as I came down the aisle, first because Brian and Mark had positioned themselves on either side of the door in case Jim Sorringer walked in, and second because of the quirky little look Lester gave me to make sure I wouldn't cry. My gown rustled softly with each step I took in my dyed teal pumps.

I had just passed Patrick when I felt the silk bag under my arm slip away. For a moment my face froze, but I knew I couldn't stop to pick it up. *Keep going,* I told myself. *Ignore it and keep going.*

Then I thought, *What if Sylvia doesn't see it and trips over it? What if . . . ?* But out of the corner of my eye I saw Patrick reach down, and I knew he would take care of it for me. *Step . . . pause . . . step . . . pause.*

I could see friends looking at me on either side of the aisle—Jill and Karen, even Amy Sheldon. Aunt Sally, of course, already had a tissue in her hand and was dabbing at one eye. A few more feet and I could smell Dad's cologne. I reached my spot across from Lester, and all of us turned expectantly toward the back of the church.

The musicians played even louder now, and then there she was, on her brother's arm. No one was standing, because the program had respectfully requested that guests remain seated during the bridal procession. As Sylvia had explained to me, there was no reason in heaven why people should stand up when the bride comes in, as though she's the queen of England or something.

I had agreed. "Besides," I'd told her, "this way *every*one can see the bride, not just the ones on the aisle."

Kirk was smiling, Sylvia was smiling—it seemed as though everyone on earth was smiling right then. Sylvia's face and neck and shoulders seemed to have taken on a soft patina, like the alabaster I'd read about in *Arabian Nights*. Her eyes weren't on anyone but my father, and Dad seemed to see no one but her. His face was so full of delight and awe that I wondered if Les would have to prompt him when it was time for his vows. He reached out for Sylvia, one arm circling her waist, and pulled her close, as though he would never, ever, let her go.

The sunlight streaming through the glass panels filled the whole sanctuary with warmth, and I felt like I was standing in the Emerald City of Oz.

"Dearly beloved . . . ," the minister began, and I let out my breath in one slow, relieved sigh.

The ceremony was an odd mixture of traditional and modern. The minister talked about the different phases of love—how Ben and Sylvia had experienced grief and separation and loneliness during their courtship, yet love had prevailed. Not the kind of love that focuses on self, he said; not the kind that demands immediate gratification, but a love built on trust and loyalty and patience and understanding. A love that can't be toppled by distance or events that postpone fulfillment. "Ben and Sylvia," he finished, "have found in each other the three elements of lasting love: passion, tenderness, and joy."

It was just then, as my eyes scanned the guests, that I saw Jim Sorringer appear in the doorway at the back of the church.

I stopped breathing. At the same moment he stepped into the sanctuary, I saw Mark and Brian glance at each other and then, like robots, move a few steps toward him and stand on either side.

Pamela and Elizabeth, in the third row, must have read something in my face, because I saw them glance hastily toward the back of the room, then forward again, their eyes huge and fixed on me. Across from me, Les raised one eyebrow. I concentrated on Dad and Sylvia again. There were no seats left. Sorringer would have to stand.

". . . with this ring, I thee wed," the minister was saying.

"With this ring," my dad repeated, slipping a wide band of white and yellow gold on Sylvia's finger, "I thee wed."

"With my body, I thee worship . . ."

"With my body, I thee worship," said my dad.

I'm not sure, but I think I blushed just then. Of all the times I had fantasized about two people in bed having sex, I had never exactly thought of it as worship. But I liked the sound of it—between Dad and Sylvia, anyway.

I stole another glance at the back of the room. I wondered how many times Jim Sorringer had worshipped Sylvia with his body. I considered casting a cold, calculating look in his direction, but I thought better of it.

All I could see of Sylvia now was the back of her head, the veil white and billowy down to her waist. I could see Dad's face, though, the tender look in his eyes as he repeated the minister's words, Lester's solemn expression.

"I, Ben, take thee, Sylvia, as wife of all my days . . ."

Then we heard Sylvia's soft voice saying her vows: "I, Sylvia, take thee, Ben, as husband of all my days . . ."

I had thought that when Sylvia was finished, the minister would pronounce them husband and wife. Instead, Sylvia turned to me and Dad turned to Lester, and each put out a hand and drew us close to them at the altar.

"Just as we welcome Sylvia into this family

circle," the minister continued, "Ben and Sylvia's love for each other encompasses Alice and Lester, too. This union is one of more than a single couple. At the end of every year may each of you be able to say to the others, 'You have brought out the best in me and made me a better person.' Together you make a family, and as a family, you make a home."

I almost lost it then. From my end of the lineup, I could hear Lester swallow and I knew that it got to him, too. But just when I thought I might cry, I heard the minister saying, "If anyone here knows a reason why these two should not be united in holy matrimony . . ."

There was a rustle and a creak, and I thought my heart had stopped beating. I couldn't help myself. I just had to glance toward the back of the sanctuary, then forward again, before I realized it was only Grandpa McKinley, impatient for the minister to get on with it.

The minister's face broke into a happy smile. "Then by the power vested in me, I now pronounce you, Ben and Sylvia, husband and wife. Ben, you may kiss your bride."

Lester and I automatically stepped aside. There wasn't the faintest creak or rustle or cough as Dad turned toward Sylvia, his hands clutching her arms. For a few seconds he just gazed into her face, and then he leaned forward, his lips lightly brushing hers. Finally he drew her to him and kissed her tenderly—a *long* kiss—before he let her go, and I saw her fingers discreetly caress the back of his neck.

The hush was almost something you could touch. The hush, the smiles, the sunlight, and then—from Pamela and Elizabeth in the third row—a soft, triumphant *"Yes!"* and the entire audience broke into applause.

6

Hearts, Broken
and Otherwise

I took Lester's arm, and we walked back up the aisle behind Dad and Sylvia as the ensemble played the last movement of the wedding composition again, full of life and joy. It seemed to me as though every bell in the universe should be ringing. I couldn't stop smiling. I was afraid I might cry at the same time, because sometimes I cry even when I'm happy.

All I did, though, was swallow, and Lester noticed.

"Don't cry," he muttered, giving my arm a shake. "Don't cry or you'll smear your mascara and end up looking like a raccoon."

I laughed then and waved to people I knew from school. We had to wait in the stone chapel at one end of the church as the guests were leaving. Most of them were heading for the reception at the Hyatt, but all the kids from school were directed to the church lounge. When the sanctuary was empty, we went back for photos. Sylvia took off her shoes, and so did I.

"I promise I'll make it quick," the photographer told us, smiling. He took shots of the bride alone, Sylvia and Dad, Sylvia and me, Dad and Sylvia and Lester and me, the four of us plus Kirk and Nancy—almost every combination you could think of.

Lois stuck her head in the chapel. "I count seventy kids out here, Sylvia. I sent one of them to the Giant for more cookies and punch, and they want to know if they can dance. One of them brought a CD player."

"Bless you, Lois," Sylvia said, slipping on her shoes again. "We'll be right out." She turned to Dad. "Could they dance for a while, do you think?"

"I don't see why not," said Dad.

When we entered the lounge, the kids all clapped and cheered, and maybe it was the first time Dad had seen just how popular a teacher Sylvia was.

"When are you coming back to school?" they kept asking her.

"First week of November," she told them.

"Oh, Alice, it was beautiful!" Elizabeth said as my own friends came crowding around. "And you're gorgeous in that dress!"

"It's really hot!" said Jill. And she actually sounded envious. Of *me*!

"*Sex-y!*" said Karen.

"What happened to Jim Sorringer?" I whispered. "One minute he was there and the next he wasn't."

"I think that long kiss was more than he could take," Brian said. "He went outside about then for a cigarette."

"When the minister asked if anyone knew why they shouldn't be married, I almost died!" said Pamela, and we all began to giggle.

"I was sure I'd turn around to see Sorringer coming down the aisle for Sylvia," I told them.

"We were ready," said Mark. "Brian and I were going to do the bouncer bit."

Patrick had been standing off to one side, smiling at me. I felt my face flush a little as he walked over. "Nice dress!" he said. "Very . . . uh . . ."

"Hot!" said Elizabeth.

"Sophisticated," said Patrick. "Here. I think you dropped something."

"My purse!" I said. "Oh, Patrick, thank you!"

"I wondered if there was anything in it you'd need up there, so I peeked. I was afraid maybe you were the one with the ring." He looked at me strangely. "What'd you do? Pig out on doughnuts before the ceremony?"

I remembered the Krispy Kreme bag I'd stuffed

in my clutch at the last minute. "No, it was supposed to be a barf bag in case Sylvia threw up."

He stared at me incredulously. "Girls think about stuff like that? I mean, you actually *plan* for somebody throwing up?"

Elizabeth and I burst out laughing. "Well, somebody has to, Patrick! You can't just let life happen to you," I said, smiling back. It felt strange to be telling Patrick Long, the world's ultimate life planner, something like that.

Dad motioned for me to come over and stand in the receiving line, even though we knew we'd have to do the same thing once we got to the reception. What was funny was how all the guys who are in high school now—Mark and Brian and Patrick and the others—took the opportunity to kiss the bride. The junior high kids who were still her students were too shy. They just stood around and giggled.

What was even funnier was that some of the guys, Patrick included, kissed me too. And he held it a few seconds longer than the others did. I smiled at him, surprised, as he straightened up again. I guess if you're standing in a receiving line, you have to be prepared for anything. But what was really hilarious was the number of girls who wanted to kiss Lester.

He did look sexy in his dark blue suit. I wasn't

sure I'd ever seen Les in a suit in my life. A sport coat, of course. Maybe even a blazer. But a suit? "Weddings and funerals only, that's my limit," he said when I asked him where he'd wear it.

Gwen and Pamela wandered over to the punch table, where the guys had gathered, the junior high boys grabbing whole handfuls of cookies at a time. I was still in the receiving line talking to Karen and Jill when I saw Elizabeth gesturing to me wildly from across the room.

I looked toward the end of the receiving line where the last five kids were standing, and there was Jim Sorringer, waiting to kiss the bride.

With my eyes, I motioned Elizabeth to get the guys, and she must have understood, because I saw her whirl around and head for Patrick and Brian. By the time she had rounded up a small fleet, Jim Sorringer had got up to me.

"Uh . . . Lester, this is Mr. Sorringer, our vice principal back in junior high school," I said, not knowing if Lester had ever met Sylvia's former boyfriend or not.

"Nice to see you again, Alice," Mr. Sorringer said, shaking my hand. "Lester . . ." He shook Lester's hand, too, but his eyes were on Sylvia.

Hurry! my eyes pleaded, watching the guys around the punch table whisper among themselves and then start toward us.

It was too late.

Sylvia turned toward the next person in line and startled when she realized it was Jim. The smile sort of froze on her face. Dad looked both pleasant and protective, as though he would allow nothing or no one to ruin this day. He put one arm around Sylvia's shoulder.

"Hello, Jim," Sylvia said, putting out her hand.

My heart was racing. I was maid of honor! I was supposed to help out! I was supposed to know what to do in emergencies to save the bride. I remembered the time I had poured my glass of 7UP down the back of an actress who had hold of Lester's pants and wouldn't let go. What should I do if Sorringer tried to grab her? Get out the barf bag and pull it over his head?

Jim reached out and took Sylvia's hand in both of his. "I saw the notice on the bulletin board that your students were invited to the ceremony, Sylvia," he said. "I hoped it applied to old boyfriends as well." Sylvia blushed slightly, and he added, "I wish you happiness every day of your life. And I want to thank you for making the time we spent together the happiest of mine."

He leaned forward then and kissed her on the cheek. I think he'd been aiming for her lips, but she turned her head slightly so that he got the side of her face.

"Thanks, Jim. I appreciate that," Sylvia said. "And I wish the very best for you."

I'll bet Sorringer had that little speech all pre-pared. Rehearsed it, even. I noticed the way his fingers squeezed her arms, but even before Patrick and Brian and Mark moved in, Jim Sorringer turned to Dad. "Congratulations, Ben," he said, giving his hand a quick shake. And then he turned and made his way through the bouncers who had gathered in case he needed an escort, and strode on out the door.

"Talk about a class act!" said Lester.

I was watching Dad and Sylvia exchange looks, saw Dad squeeze her shoulder.

"All except that line about the time they'd spent together," I murmured to Les. But Mr. Sorringer *hadn't* tried to ruin the wedding. He *hadn't* made a scene. It suddenly occurred to me that I didn't have any huge worries at the moment. Dad and Sylvia were married, I hadn't tripped or stumbled, Nancy was recovering even though she couldn't be in the ceremony, Lester was living close by, and life was good.

When the last student had passed through the receiving line, Sylvia gave a huge sigh and turned, smiling, to me. "Well?" she said, and we laughed together.

"Mom?" I said, and we hugged.

"Call me whatever seems natural," she said. "'Sylvia' will do."

I'm glad she said that, because I'm not sure I could ever get used to calling her "Mom."

Dad just beamed. "Well, are we ready to head off to the reception and do this all over again?" he asked.

"Why don't we go on ahead, Ben, and let Alice have a little more time with her friends," Sylvia said. "Lois is going to look after things here, and she'll drive her over."

"Good idea," said Dad.

I ducked in the rest room to check my makeup and see if I still looked as glamorous and adult as I had that morning. I'd just turned toward the mirror when I thought I heard a sob from one of the stalls. The door was ajar, and Lori suddenly emerged, blowing her nose on a piece of toilet paper. She hadn't heard me come in and quickly looked away.

"Lori?" I said.

The tall girl turned back again and faked a smile. "It was a beautiful wedding, Alice," she said.

I looked at her closely. "What's the matter?"

She pretended to give her hair a quick inspection. "Nothing," she said.

"Come on, Lori. What is it?" I persisted.

And suddenly her face crumpled and she covered

it with both hands. "Leslie and I broke up," she said, and leaned against the sink, sobbing.

"Oh, Lori! I'm . . . I'm really sorry!" I said, and gave her a hug.

"She's going out with someone else," Lori cried, backing away then. "We were so *right* for each other, Alice! We had all these plans. . . ." She cried all the harder.

What do you say to someone who has just had her heart broken? What could anyone have said that would have helped me when Patrick and I broke up? Nothing. You have to get yourself through it, that's all.

"She was your first real girlfriend, right?" I said, trying to think of something to put it in perspective.

Lori blew her nose. "Oh, I know what you're thinking, Alice. That it was only puppy love."

"I'm not thinking that at all, Lori," I told her. "I'll bet you're feeling just as bad as I did when Patrick and I split up. All I can say is that there are more loves in your future. You just haven't found them yet." It sounded so trite.

Lori blew her nose a second time. She looked really good in her beige pants and top, as stylish as a New York model. "It's not as easy for us, Alice."

"I guess not," I said.

Amy Sheldon came in just then, and Lori dabbed at her eyes with a paper towel. "Go on out," she murmured to me. "I'm okay."

I hesitated.

"It was just seeing how happy your dad is with Sylvia that made me all the more miserable," she said, smiling a little.

"I sure know how *that* feels!" I said.

"Listen," said Lori, "I need a tampon. Do you have one, Alice?"

"No," I told her.

"I do," Amy called from inside the stall, and when she came out she said, "I always take one with me wherever I go. Here."

"Thanks, Amy," said Lori, and took it into a stall.

"I figure if I don't need it, someone else will," Amy continued.

"Thanks, Amy," I said.

"And see? You were lucky I was here."

"Thanks, Amy," called Lori.

"If you want another one, just let me know."

"Thanks, Amy," I told her.

She finally got the message and left. Lori peeked out the door. "Is she gone?" she whispered, and we laughed.

"Poor Amy," I said. Then, "Come on." I grabbed Lori's hand and pulled her into the lounge, where the kids were now dancing. I was glad to see Amy Sheldon right in the middle of things too, even though she was dancing all by herself.

I turned Lori around, facing me. "Let's dance," I said, and she looked at me, all smiles. Then Gwen and Elizabeth joined in, then Amy, and soon we had a whole group of us dancing together, just us girls.

Love sure is complicated, I thought. With all that was going on at home and at school, it was a perfect time for me to be going solo, and I intended to enjoy every minute of my sophomore year.

But a few minutes later when I went out to the water fountain in the hall, Elizabeth followed me and grabbed my arm. "Listen, Alice, you're going to kill me, I know . . ."

I straightened up slowly, water dripping from my chin. *Now what?*

She had an agonized look on her face. "Ross called me this morning. His brother is driving to D.C. today to look over George Washington University, and Ross asked if he could come along and see me. He'll only be here for a short time—a couple of hours, maybe. I didn't want to tell you before the wedding because I was afraid you'd be upset. Would you be mad at me forever if I skipped the reception?"

I blinked. The wedding of the century, practi-

cally, that we'd all been waiting for forever, and
Liz, one of my best friends, wouldn't be at the
reception? And then, in Elizabeth's eyes, the *guy*
of the century and one of the few chances she had
to see him . . .

"Of course not, Liz!" I said. "It's great you can
get together. Go ahead."

"Oh, Alice!" she said, and hugged me.

We went back in the lounge, where Patrick was
dancing with the others. I went over and started
dancing in front of him, grabbing onto his shoulders.

"Hey!" he said, looking down at me in surprise
and smiling.

"Hey!" I said. "Would you be willing to fill in for
one of the girls?"

"Huh?" said Patrick.

"I invited Liz and Pamela and Gwen to my dad's
reception, but Elizabeth's boyfriend is coming to
town this afternoon. She can't go. Will you?"

Patrick put his hands on my waist and went on
smiling and dancing. "Do I have to wear a dress?"
he asked.

I just laughed. "No."

"Will there be food?"

"Fabulous food."

"How long?"

"Couple hours, maybe. You can leave anytime.
After you dance with me, that is."

"Okay. I'll have to call my folks and tell them where to pick me up," he said.

I smiled after him as he went to find a phone and wondered if I really wanted to go solo my sophomore year or not.

7

I Could Have Danced All Night

The four of us—Patrick, Gwen, Pamela, and me—rode to the reception with Lois. We went into a large private room at the Hyatt, where eight tables had been set for ten each, with tablecloths alternating among royal blue, teal, and ivory. Dad's composer friend and his ensemble were playing off to one side when I came in, and—mercifully—I'd missed the receiving line.

People were milling about with drinks in their hands when Lester took the microphone and invited everyone to find their places at the tables. I went up to the head table with Dad and Sylvia and Nancy and Kirk and my two uncles, as waiters went around pouring champagne in all the glasses. Lester tried to get everyone's attention again, but a lot of people were talking, so Uncle Howard took his fork and tapped it gently against his water glass. Amazing how a high-pitched tapping sound like that can quiet people down.

"Welcome, everyone," Lester said again. "I'd like to make a toast to my dad, and I'll start off by saying what a great choice he made in choosing Sylvia Summers to be his wife." People smiled and so did Dad. "The ceremony we witnessed this morning couldn't have happened to a better man." Everyone applauded. "And I want Sylvia to know that Alice and I welcome her into our family and will do our best to make her feel loved and cherished, as I know she feels with Dad. This is October, but a line from an old Celtic song describes how we feel about Sylvia Summers joining our family: 'The summer is a comin' in and winter's gone away, oh!'" More applause, more smiles from Dad and Sylvia. Then Lester raised his champagne glass and said, "To Dad and Sylvia, may your life together be as happy as you've made the rest of us right now."

All the guests lifted their glasses and said, "To Ben and Sylvia." Aunt Sally cried, and half the people at the tables were tearing up, myself included. I saw Sylvia lean over and hug Lester when he sat back down. Dad had said I could have a little champagne, so I took a few sips and tried not to bawl.

Then the waiters arrived with platters of food

and served each person individually—crab cakes and lobster salad and little sandwiches made with filet mignon. I don't think Dad and Sylvia ate much because they kept getting up to walk around the room and talk to people. Lester managed to get them back to the table finally so they could eat a little more. At a table in one corner Gwen and Pamela and Patrick began clinking their knives against their glasses, and then we all joined in. We wanted Sylvia and Dad to kiss, so they did.

At last Mr. Parks, the guys' P.E. teacher at Sylvia's junior high, took over the role of deejay for the afternoon.

"And now," he said at the microphone, "please welcome the new Mr. and Mrs. Ben McKinley, dancing to their song, 'All the Things You Are.'"

I didn't know Dad and Sylvia had a song! They moved out onto the floor while everyone clapped, and a lot of people began taking pictures of them. The trio played this final song before they left— the rest of the music would come from CDs—and Sylvia seemed to fit in Dad's arms like fingers in a glove, as though she belonged in those arms and had been there all her life.

Not only didn't I know Dad and Sylvia had a song, I didn't even know the song. But then Mr. Parks started singing it, and I didn't know he could sing! He had a good voice, actually, and the words told about all the things that Sylvia was to Dad and he was to her—springtime and stars and angel glow—and how happy they would be when they belonged to each other. If I cried any more, I thought, my mascara would be all over my face.

But somehow I managed to control myself, and soon I was out on the floor dancing with my dad, looking at him smile down at me, while Les danced with Sylvia. After that I had so many partners, I didn't even keep count. I know I danced with Kirk and Uncle Milt and Uncle Harold and Uncle Howard. I even did a dance with Grandpa McKinley. I faced the wheelchair, grasped the arms, and turned it back and forth in time to the music. At first Grandpa looked at me as though I had risen up out of the sea, but then he started to laugh, and that made us all happy.

As soon as I could, I went over to the table where Patrick and Gwen and Pamela were sitting to catch my breath.

"It's like being back in junior high!" said Pamela. "Look at all the teachers here!"

"I saw the principal," I said, nodding toward Mr. Ormand. "And Mrs. Pinotti—she's so tiny, you blink your eyes and you'd miss her. Who else?"

"Mr. Tawes, Mrs. Whipple . . . ," said Gwen.

"Oh my God!" I whispered. "There's Mrs. Bolino. Do you remember her, Pamela? The Our Changing Bodies unit?"

"Of course. And it was all over school what you did! She said we should be proud of our sex, so you held your female organs diagram to your chest and she said you had to wear it for the rest of the period."

"And you wore it all day!" added Gwen. "Everyone was staring at you. I didn't know you so well then. I thought you were a little crazy."

We were all laughing. I could see Patrick's ears turning pink, so I said, "And you took a look at my diagram, Patrick, and said I had missed the cervix, and I was so embarrassed." Maybe the champagne had gone to my head.

His ears *were* pink. "Yeah, I thought she was a little nuts too," he said to Gwen.

"Look!" Pamela said. "Mr. Everett!"

That really got our attention. I don't know how we had missed him. He was the handsomest teacher who ever taught junior high. He was our eighth-grade health instructor who won a couple of "best teacher" awards, and he deserved every one of them.

"I'm going to ask Mr. Everett to dance," said Pamela.

"You wouldn't!" said Gwen.

"She would," I said. "Just watch her."

Pamela always did like a dare. She got up and made her way around the tables. But just as she got to Mr. Everett, he and Mrs. Bolino started toward the dance floor.

"Oh, Pamela!" he said. "Say, save the next dance for me, okay?"

She was embarrassed, I could tell, but as she turned to come back Mr. Hensley stopped her and said, "Pamela, may I have this dance instead?"

"Uh-oh," said Patrick. "Horse-Breath Hensley." It was sad but true—our old seventh-grade World Studies teacher had the worst breath of anyone we knew, and he also spit when he talked.

Gwen covered her eyes. "Can you hold your breath for three minutes and still live?" she asked.

It would be terrible to be remembered for your breath, I thought. Mr. Hensley wasn't the most exciting teacher we'd ever had, but he was fair. And it was in his class that we buried a time capsule out in the schoolyard, and we're all supposed to come back when we're sixty years old for the opening-up ceremony.

As we watched, though, Mr. Hensley proved to be an excellent dancer. Who would have thought? Here he was, retired and boring, and yet he looked as though he was born to be on a dance floor. We could tell that Pamela was surprised.

"Look at her face!" I said. "She's absolutely staring at him!" In and out of the dancers they went. I don't know what dance it was, because I never was a very good dancer. A fox-trot? You couldn't prove it by me. But they made a great pair! And when the dance was over, Mr. Everett asked Pamela to dance next, and one of the younger men came over and asked Gwen.

Patrick looked at me. "Guess we're the only ones left."

"Yeah," I said. "Too bad for you."

He just reached across the table, put his hand over mine, then stood up. I followed him out on the dance floor, and we were both a little embarrassed when the deejay put on a really slow number.

Patrick put one arm around me and held my hand up close to his chest. He didn't say anything, just smiled down at me, and I was astonished at how much taller he had gotten. I swear, he must have grown an inch each semester. Did I fit in his arms like Sylvia fit into Dad's? I wondered. All I knew was that he was holding me pretty darn close, and I put my cheek against his chest. I knew that Patrick was serious about getting through high school in three years. I knew he had big plans for college, for life. I knew that he didn't have time for a girlfriend. But I also felt like I was special to him somehow—Patrick in his dark blue sport coat and tan pants and bright red tie. I wanted in the worst way to find out what he had told Penny after she asked him out and whether that was still on for the evening, but I didn't. Why ruin a wonderful day?

"Sort of nice to be dancing together again, isn't it?" he said.

I smiled up at him. "Oh, it's probably that old 'first girlfriend syndrome,'" I said. "You know— you never forget your first love."

He grinned. "How do you know you were the first?"

I laughed. "You mean I wasn't? How many girls were there, Patrick?"

He appeared to be silently counting. "Well, there was Grandma, my mom, my aunt . . ."

We both laughed. And then, too soon, the music was over. Patrick gave my hand a little squeeze and led me back to the table.

Mr. Everett came over and asked me to dance. I guess when a teacher knows he's a hottie, he makes sure to pay equal attention to all his former students; and since there were only three of us younger girls here, he did it graciously enough. I wished I could have danced better. I stumbled over his feet at least twice, and both times he apologized, as though it were his fault.

"Big day for your dad, huh?" he said to me. Mr. Everett is a giant, practically—six feet five or six. The top of my head only reached his chest, and I had to look way up to see him, like sitting in the first row of a movie theater or something.

"We've been waiting for this day for a long time," I told him. What I wanted to say was, *Yeah, we were scared Mr. Sorringer would ruin it, but Sylvia chose the best man.*

"Did Mrs. Everett come too?" I asked. I couldn't remember if he was sitting with a woman or not.

"No, our three-year-old has a fever, so Brin is with her today," he said. "In fact, this is my last dance, and then I have to go. But Sylvia's one of our favorite teachers, and I really wanted to be here to help celebrate."

"And you're the other favorite teacher," I said, but he just chuckled.

Most of the music, I realized, was slow, danceable music—with a partner, I mean. Now and then Mr. Parks threw in a fast number for the younger crowd, but mainly it was the kind of music Dad and Sylvia liked.

You know what's really weird, though? At least two more teachers—Mr. Tawes and Mr. Kessler—danced with me. The weirdest feeling in the whole world is to be holding hands with the teacher who taught you math or earth science, his hand on your waist as though you were a grown lady. I decided that if any of them tried to dance cheek to cheek, I would check out of there fast, but none of them did. They just asked me how high school was going and everything. I'll bet they all envied my dad.

Marilyn was there too, with Jack, her fiancé. I had hoped I would see sparks between her and Lester. I had almost hoped that Lester would cut in and waltz her right out of the room. But Marilyn danced with her head dreamily on Jack's shoulder, and Lester spent most of his time with Carol. Some things, I guess, weren't meant to be. I was having a great time, though, and could have danced all night.

Except that it wasn't night, it was afternoon, and the cake was being cut. People were gathering around again, then dancing again, then watching Lester and Carol teach the rest of us a new dance. I don't know what it was called—the Slither or something—but Les and Carol sort of slunk across the floor sideways like mobsters, Les behind Carol with his hands on her waist in one direction, Carol behind Les going the other way.

I took off my shoes at last and sat down with Gwen and Pamela, happy to watch everyone else dance for a while. Patrick came off the dance floor finally to thank me for inviting him, and then he left about the same time Mr. Everett did, so it was just us girls again. I was glad Patrick had been able to stay as long as he did, since he hadn't planned on the reception. But I couldn't help wondering if he wasn't going out with Penny later.

"Don't tell *me* Patrick doesn't still like you, girl," Gwen said. She looked good in a rose-colored dress, the skirt in filmy layers. "He was watching you even when you weren't looking at him."

I just smiled. "Well, it was nice having him here. Have you heard from Joe?" I asked, wondering about the guy she'd met at camp last summer.

"Now and then," she said. "But this semester I'm dating my books."

"You and Patrick both," I said.

I noticed that Uncle Howard and Uncle Harold were carrying gifts out to their car—presents that had been brought to the reception and needed to be taken back to the house. But it wasn't until I saw Dad and Sylvia slowly making their way to the door, a crowd around them, that I realized they were leaving.

Everyone gathered near the entrance to see them off, and I picked up my shoes and went along with the crowd. I wanted to hug Dad and Sylvia and explain that they'd be getting my present later. But it would seem awkward to push my way through all the people, and I was sure Dad would look around for Les and me and signal us to come over. So I just waited and smiled as friends made little jokes and gave them their best wishes.

The four men in front of me must have been music instructors at the Melody Inn, because they broke into some kind of a good-bye song in German—a German drinking song, maybe, judging by the way they kept raising their beer mugs at the end of each phrase. Some of the other guests joined in.

I finally backed up and went around the edge of the room, away from the crowd, until I could reach the door that way, but when I stepped outside, I saw Dad's car, newly washed and polished, just moving out the end of the driveway and into the Saturday traffic.

I stared after them—hurt and stunned. Dad left on his honeymoon with the woman I had found for him, and he didn't even hug me? Thank me? Tell me good-bye? Dad *always* tells me good-bye. Even when he goes to work in the mornings, he always says something special. What did they do—tell everyone else they were leaving except me, the Girl Who Brought Them Together? What was I? Just some leftover deviled egg on the hors d'oeuvres platter?

Tears came to my eyes. I couldn't stop them. Pamela and Gwen had gone to the rest room, and I searched blindly around the room until I found Lester having a beer over by a window.

"Whoa!" he said when I collided with the back of his suit coat. He grabbed at my hand.

"Dad . . . ," was all I could say.

"Nope. I don't know what you're drinking, Al, but it's me . . . Les," he said, waving one hand in front of my face.

"H-H-He didn't even tell me good-bye!" I choked out.

"He didn't?" Lester looked thoughtful. "Well, he didn't tell me good-bye either. I know they're try-ing to make it to the Greenbrier before it gets dark, and it's at least a four-hour drive."

"Well, what's going to happen to *me*?" I asked desperately. "Nobody's said."

"Hey, Al, you're not an orphan," said Les.

"No one tells me anything! Carol's staying at your place, and Nancy and Lois are staying at Sylvia's, and—"

"Aunt Sally and Uncle Milt are going to stay with you till Dad and Sylvia get back," he said.

"Aunt *Sally*!" I bleated, and Lester hushed me before I attracted attention. "You get Carol, and Dad gets Sylvia, and I get Aunt *Sally*? Why didn't Dad just send me to Girl Scout camp? A convent?"

"Shhhh," said Lester. "Tell you what, why don't you invite Gwen and Pamela to stay with you, over the weekend at least? If Aunt Sally objects, tell her you got it straight from the horse's mouth."

That was a little better. It's not that I don't love

Aunt Sally. I do, in a relative sort of way, and we were certain to eat well while she was at our place. But she's not exactly Fun City. You would hardly call being with Aunt Sally a blast.

I did manage to mind my manners and thank Margaret and her mother for doing my hair and makeup.

"And you looked great," Margaret said. She looked great herself, a little too much like a lawyer, maybe, in a gray silk outfit, almost like her mother's, but semi-great, anyway. And she *did* know a lot about makeup.

"Good-bye," I said to Kirk when he told me they were flying back that evening. "It's nice to meet Sylvia's side of the family. It was a treat to see both you and Nancy."

"And now that we know Sylvia is in good hands and that Nancy's getting well, it will be a better year for all of us," Kirk said.

The reception ended a half hour later as people began to drift off and waiters came in to clear the tables. Pamela said she could stay with me over the weekend, but Gwen's dad was celebrating his birthday, so she had to get home. Her mom was already parked outside.

Nancy was tired and needed to lie down. Lois drove her back to Sylvia's house on Saul Road, then drove Pamela to her house and me to mine, where Aunt Sally and Uncle Milt were already unpacking up in Dad and Sylvia's bedroom. Before I went upstairs, I picked up the hall phone and called Elizabeth. I told her Pamela was coming over later to spend the weekend and asked if she could come.

"Yes, if you promise not to speculate every minute about what your dad and Sylvia are doing," Elizabeth said.

I laughed. "Can we speculate on what you and *Ross* were doing this afternoon?" I asked. Then *she* laughed.

I went upstairs to change out of my teal dress and put on my jeans and fleece top. I wanted to get off all the makeup and be me again. I decided that the first thing I wanted to do when Liz and Pamela came over was to go walking around the neighborhood, kicking through dry leaves. Forgetting that Dad and Sylvia had left without telling me good-bye.

I slipped off the dress, and as I laid it across the bed, I saw a small box on my bedspread with a note beside it.

I opened the box first. Inside was a delicate bracelet, small jade stones set in silver. I unfolded the note:

Dear Alice,
Thank you for being my brides-
maid, my maid of honor, and—
most of all—my new daughter. I'm
looking forward to getting to know
you even better when we get back.
Love,
Sylvia

"Oh, Alice, you're back!" Aunt Sally said, stopping in the doorway. "I see you found the little box. Sylvia gave it to me before she and Ben left and asked me to give it to you. Now, isn't that beautiful."

Yes, it was. I smiled.

8

A Bedroom Surprise

As soon as Aunt Sally got downstairs, she started cooking something. Uncle Milt stretched out on the couch to nap until suppertime, which gave Elizabeth and Pamela and me a chance to go outside and walk around the neighborhood and talk.

"So tell me *every*thing!" Elizabeth insisted. "Did your dad and Sylvia have a song? Did Lester give a toast? Did anyone hit on you, Pamela?"

We did tell her everything—Jim Sorringer, Mr. Everett, Mr. Hensley, Lester and Carol and the Slither, the food, Patrick and me. . . .

"Now *you* tell us everything," I said. "What did you and Ross do? Where did you meet?"

"I took the Metro downtown and met him at a Starbucks near GW," Elizabeth said. "His brother was looking over the campus, so we had about two hours—they're driving back this evening. We talked and talked and—"

"Kissed and kissed," said Pamela.

"That, too," said Elizabeth, her eyes smiling. But she looked wistful. "He says he wants me to go out with other guys. That it wouldn't be fair for me not to. That he can't come down every time there's a dance or a good movie or a basketball game or something."

We were quiet, knowing what that meant—that he'd be going out with girls up there in Pennsylvania. "But we still had a good time together," Elizabeth said. "We walked around the GW neighborhood, and he said he might be able to get down now and then after he gets his license, especially if his brother makes the university." Then she added, "If we got really serious about each other, I wonder how this would turn out. If we'd agree to wait for each other."

"Too bad we can't sort of freeze-dry Ross and defrost him when you're both twenty-four," I said. "Love gets complicated, you know?"

We turned a corner and saw a maple tree, totally gorgeous with green and yellow and orange leaves, all on the same tree. We walked and talked a long time—about the wedding, about love, Lester, Lori, life. . . .

I hadn't told either Elizabeth or Pamela about my conversation with Lori in the rest room at the church, but Pamela had heard about the breakup from Karen, who was spreading the news by e-mail. Pamela said there had been a message waiting for her when she'd gone home to change.

"Do you suppose it's the same as breaking up with a guy?" Pamela asked.

"Why not?" I said.

Elizabeth, in her blue sweats, thrust her hands deep in her jacket pockets. "I don't know. I can't imagine it. I mean, kissing another girl is sort of like kissing yourself. Where's the thrill in that?"

We thought about that awhile.

"Maybe," I said, "but haven't you ever wondered what a girl sees in some particular guy who doesn't interest you at all?"

"Sure."

"Well, maybe it's the same for lesbians. They see things in some other girl that may not attract you in the least. But Lori's really hurting right now. I think she liked Leslie a lot."

"Who did Leslie ditch her for?" Elizabeth asked.

"Someone from another school, I heard," said Pamela. "I think he met Leslie at a church conference or something."

Elizabeth and I both reacted at once: "*He*? A *guy*?"

"According to Karen."

"Wow." Elizabeth let out her breath and walked noisily through a large pile of leaves against the curb. Pamela and I followed, kicking them high in the air and letting them fall again on our feet. "I've heard that there's someone in the world for every single person alive," Elizabeth said. "It's just that some of them never find each other. Isn't that depressing? What if they find each other, like Ross and me, only it's not the right time?"

Pamela shrugged. "What about people who want to stay single?" Then she muttered, "*I* know two people who should have stayed single. My parents." Pamela's mom has been gone for two years, but now she's back here in Maryland again, wanting to be part of the family, and Mr. Jones won't take her back.

"If they'd stayed single, Pamela, we wouldn't have *you*!" I told her, and slipped one arm around her waist.

We strolled by the playground of our old elementary school, where we hang out sometimes, but nobody was there, so we started back home again. I studied our house as we got closer, as though seeing it for the first time. Just an ordinary two-story house, but with Dad and Sylvia gone, it was the one familiar thing I could count on. Then I remembered.

"Did you know Sylvia wants to remodel our house?" I said. "She wants to enlarge their bedroom, put in a master bath, and add a study downstairs. They'd use Lester's old room for a guest room."

"Privacy," said Elizabeth. "You can hardly blame her."

"It's only natural," said Pamela. "By the way, where's your cousin Carol staying while she's in town? I figured she would be staying with you."

"She's at Lester's," I said.

Elizabeth stopped in her tracks. "With three guys?"

"That's Carol!" I said.

"And using the same bathroom?" cried Elizabeth.

Pamela grinned. "Not all at the same time," she told her.

We had a late supper of soup and corn bread, and later, when we were in my room again, Aunt Sally brought up a huge metal bowl of popcorn.

"You sure make a good mom," I told her. She was pleased.

"Have some," Elizabeth offered, holding out the bowl for Aunt Sally, and she smiled as she sat down on the edge of my bed and took a handful, thrilled, I think, to be included.

I got out the sheet and pillowcase set I was working on for Dad and Sylvia and let Aunt Sally exclaim over it.

"Now, isn't that pretty!" she said. "Why, those are

the very colors Sylvia chose for her wedding!" Good old Aunt Sally. She didn't tell me that she could see where the stitches began and ended and that one of the pillowcases was wrinkled and slightly dirty.

"I know they will like that," she said. "It was a nice wedding, wasn't it?"

I nodded. "I was thinking of all the things that *weren't* perfect about it, and yet it didn't really matter, did it?" I began working on the embroidery as we talked, running a needle under the fabric and bringing it up just before the end of the stitch behind it.

"Like what wasn't perfect?" asked Elizabeth.

"Nancy not feeling well enough to be in the ceremony, Grandpa getting restless, Jim Sorringer showing up, me dropping my purse . . ."

"The biggest mistake a bride can make is thinking that everything ought to be perfect on her wedding day," said Aunt Sally emphatically. "It never is, and it just makes her upset and nervous."

Pamela grinned as she reached for the popcorn again. "What about her wedding *night*?"

"Well, now!" Aunt Sally said, and quickly pushed some popcorn in her mouth.

We could tell she was embarrassed, and Pamela said, "Erase! Erase!"

But we had invited my aunt to have popcorn

with us, and I could tell she wanted so much to be "one of the girls." "Oh," she said, blushing, "I was so stupid when I married. That's really all I can call it: stupid."

We sat awkwardly waiting, wondering what to say.

"Why?" I asked finally.

"Well," she said, lowering her voice, even though Uncle Milt had gone to bed a half hour before, "I had just thought that Milt and I could get to know each other a little better first."

I paused with the needle in my hand. "What was it, an arranged marriage or something? You'd hardly even met?"

Aunt Sally laughed a little. "No, but we'd known each other only eight months and—"

"Eight months!" Pamela cried. "Eight months, for us, is a lifetime!"

Aunt Sally was really blushing now. "Well, we weren't what you'd call 'intimate' before we married. Marie and I didn't have any brothers, you know, so I wasn't used to sharing a bathroom with a man, much less my bed! I just thought we'd do it . . . gradually, you know."

"Do it *gradually*?" Elizabeth said, astonished.

"Yeah, could you sort of describe that?" Pamela said.

Now Aunt Sally was blushing furiously. She has

pale, freckled skin—like Mom had, I'll bet—and you can always tell when she is either embarrassed or angry. "What I *meant* was . . . ," she began. "Well, I thought we could gradually get used to undressing in front of each other first, then lying in each other's arms, then some night, when we both felt ready . . ."

Pamela was frankly staring now. "No offense," she said, "but you sound like Queen Victoria's sister!"

"I know. I always was the family prude, Marie used to say," said Aunt Sally.

"I don't think that means you're a prude at all," Elizabeth told her. "I sort of feel the same way, that I might not want to 'do it' right away."

"Are you kidding? I'll want to do it the minute the wedding's over, if we haven't been 'intimate' before," said Pamela.

Elizabeth flopped over on her side. "That's what I just can't stand. All those people at the wedding staring at you and imagining what you're going to be doing that night. It's indecent! It's nobody's business! I'd just like to prove them all wrong."

"So you're going to come back from your honeymoon wearing a T-shirt that says, 'Ha-ha! I'm still a virgin'?" Pamela asked.

"Well, I know how Aunt Sally feels, because I

used to think that people only had sex when they wanted a baby. I didn't know they did it just for fun."

"Oh, my!" said Aunt Sally, and even her neck was red. "We never even used 'sex' and 'fun' in the same sentence."

"How *did* you describe it?" I asked. I was learning more about Aunt Sally than I ever thought she would tell me.

She thought about that a minute. "Beautiful . . . necessary . . . generous . . . dutiful. . . . Oh, I wish I had been more relaxed about it. It would have made it so much easier for Milt. He was so patient, though. It must be nice to feel so free and easy and natural, the way you girls do."

Natural? I thought. *Free and easy?* I wonder why grown-ups think it's so easy for us, being ourselves. Sometimes being natural and free and easy is really the hardest thing in the world.

When we woke Sunday morning, Aunt Sally was already up making French toast, and Uncle Milt was squeezing the oranges for juice.

"Hey, I think we'll hire you to stay on," I joked, giving him a hug.

"You know, Alice," he said, "you walk into a room and I see your mother. She wore her hair down to her shoulders just like you. Same color—

a little lighter, maybe. Same smile. She even walks like her mother, doesn't she, Sal?"

Aunt Sally nodded as she set the syrup on the table. "I see Marie in her all the time. But she has a new mother now, Milt, and we can't keep on talking about Marie so much."

"Sylvia wouldn't mind," I told them. "She really wouldn't. She doesn't mind if Dad talks about Mom either."

"Wise woman," Uncle Milt said.

What surprised me—bothered me, I guess— was that there were five or six pills lined up beside Uncle Milt's glass of orange juice. I looked at the pills and then at him. When had he gotten so many lines on his forehead? I'd swear they hadn't been there the last time I visited them in Chicago. Did some people just grow old all of a sudden, or was I noticing things now I hadn't seen before?

Up in my room later Pamela, Elizabeth, and I decided to paint our fingernails and toenails with a new polish Elizabeth had bought. In one kind of light it looked cobalt blue. In another, it looked black. All three of us were sitting in a row on my bed, resting against the headboard, our feet propped up on pillows, when the phone rang. I could hear Uncle Milt answering in the hall below, and though I couldn't make out what he was saying, I knew by the tone of his voice that he was confused. Then he called up the stairs: "Alice? Phone call for Pamela."

"We'll get it," I said, lifting my feet off the pillow and swiveling around until they were both on the floor. I went out in the hall. "Okay, I've got it," I called back. I took the upstairs phone off the stand outside my door and brought it into the bedroom. I handed it to Pamela as Uncle Milt hung up downstairs.

We knew the minute we heard the voice at the other end that it was Pamela's mom. As always, Pamela held the phone out away from her ear so we could hear. I think she feels we don't believe just how upsetting her mom can be.

"How did you know I was here?" Pamela said, giving us the look that meant, *Here it comes!*

"I just guessed," her mom said. "Your father said you weren't there, and even though he lies through his teeth, I figured Alice would know where you were. And, anyway, I knew her dad got married yesterday. How was the wedding?"

"It was nice," Pamela said, her voice flat.

"It's good to know that *some*one can find love the second time around," her mother went on. "I can't even get your father to believe that I never really stopped loving him and that just because I made a horrible mistake once, I shouldn't have to be treated like dogshit for the rest of my life."

Mrs. Jones does that. She'll make some reference to a current event and then relate it to everything that's happened in her own life.

"Mom, have you been drinking?" Pamela asked.

"See? See what I mean? A mother can't even call her own daughter and ask about a wedding, to which the mother wasn't invited, without people asking if she's a drunk."

"Because, if you have," Pamela continued, "I'd rather not talk with you right now." I could tell that Pamela was struggling not to either cry or lose her temper.

"So *you* don't want to talk to me? Your dad's really sold you a bill of goods, hasn't he?" Mrs. Jones wasn't exactly slurring her words, but she sounded different.

"What I want is for you to treat me like your daughter and not a girlfriend. I don't want to know what goes on between you and Dad, Mom. I just want to stay out of it."

"How the hell can I treat you like a daughter if we're not even living under the same roof?" Mrs. Jones said. And then her voice softened as she asked, "Pamela, why don't you come and visit me sometime? I'm right on a bus line. I've given you my address, but you've never come by."

"I thought you got a job at Nordstrom, Mom."

"Well, I did, but I don't work twenty-four hours

a day." I think she belched then. It sounded like a belch.

"Well, I will sometime," Pamela said.

"Promise?" said her mother.

"I'll come," said Pamela.

Lester and Carol came for lunch. Aunt Sally had been cooking all morning, and Lester claimed he could tell that Aunt Sally was in the house the minute he opened the front door. Aunt Sally is never happier than when she has a whole bunch of people around a table. I think she also figured that whatever Carol had been doing that she shouldn't, at least she couldn't do it here.

Carol herself is glamorous in a New York City kind of way. I've never even been to New York City, so maybe I don't know what I'm talking about, but I'll bet Carol could be a big-time model if she wanted.

She's got Uncle Milt's arched eyebrows, light shoulder-length hair turned under at the ends, and dimples. No woman should be allowed to be that pretty! I think Lester's had a secret crush on her since he was a little boy.

"Mmm. Smells good, Mom. All I've had this morning is coffee and half a bagel," Carol said, giving her parents hugs.

"Come by for dinner too, and I'll have a ham ready," Aunt Sally promised.

"She can't," said Lester, digging into the potato salad. "Carol's got a heavy date."

"*That* was quick!" said Uncle Milt.

"Now, Carol, who could you possibly have met in two days that you're going on a date with?" asked Aunt Sally.

"Paul Sorenson, one of my roommates," Lester said. "He and Carol hit it off, and he's going to show her Washington, D.C."

"She already knows Washington, D.C.! She's seen it with me!" her mother protested.

"Mom!" Carol chided affectionately.

"Paul's a nice guy, Sal. Even you would like him," Les said.

"Bring him by for dinner, then, and let *us* meet him," Aunt Sally said.

"I don't know him *that* well," said Carol.

"I don't understand dating today," said Aunt Sally. "How can you know him well enough to sleep in his apartment and go out on the town with him but not well enough to bring him here to meet your parents?"

"Mom, we're just going to dinner and a club or two. We're not engaged! I just met him!" Carol said, and we knew it was time to change the subject.

Pamela looked Les over. "You looked studly yesterday, Les," she said.

"I assume that's a compliment?" said Lester.

"He looked *what*?" asked Aunt Sally.

"Mature," said Les, and kissed Aunt Sally on the cheek.

I'd managed to talk to enough kids after the wedding that I got at least a few suggestions to turn in to the newspaper staff on Monday.

> *Things students feel they need to learn before they leave high school:*
> *1. Learn to pronounce Spanish words correctly even if you can't speak the language*
> *2. Put on eyeliner properly*
> *3. Get a fake ID*
> *4. Talk to your parents without arguing*
> *5. Figure out how to tell if you have bad breath*
> *6. Unhook a girl's bra*
> *7. Deal with a teacher who's sarcastic*

I left the list in the newspaper office before I went to lunch. In the cafeteria everyone told me how great I'd looked in the teal dress, everyone except Penny, of course, who—I noticed—ate at another table. I kept watching her and then

Patrick, when he came in later and sat down, to see if I could detect any sign that they'd gone out on Saturday, but I couldn't tell a thing. Maybe the date had fizzled. Or maybe it had *sizzled,* and they were keeping it all under wraps. In any case, Patrick smiled over at me and I smiled back.

Amy Sheldon sat down to eat with us too. I hoped she didn't think that just because I had invited her on impulse to Dad's wedding, it automatically made her one of our gang.

What the girls wanted to talk about, of course, was Sylvia and the dress and the honeymoon. What the guys wanted to talk about was the football game they had watched after they had gone home and whether or not the Terps—the University of Maryland's team—should keep their coach.

"Someday," Elizabeth said, speaking of Sylvia, "that will be one of us coming down the aisle."

"Who do you suppose will get married first?" Pamela said.

We looked around the table with mischievous eyes.

"Jill!" said Karen.

"Who will marry last?" said Elizabeth.

"No," said Jill. "Who'll be an old maid?"

And without even thinking, I said, "Amy!" Everyone laughed.

Did you ever say something you instantly wished you could take back? The look on Amy's face just then . . .

"So maybe I don't even want to get married," she said, looking down at her Swiss cheese sandwich.

"Of course," I said quickly, "she could become vice president of a blue-chip company." I smiled at her.

She smiled back, but her smile couldn't disguise the fact that she'd known exactly what I'd meant.

Would apologizing make it better or worse? Would inviting her to go somewhere or do something with me erase the insult? When would I discover that there isn't a delete key to press when it comes to life?

Sylvia's sister had already flown back to New Mexico. My uncles Harold and Howard, along with my aunts and Grandpa McKinley, had driven back to Tennessee the day after the wedding. Carol had gone home on Monday, and only Aunt Sally and Uncle Milt were left. They were leaving early Wednesday morning before I went to school, as Dad and Sylvia were coming home that evening. Aunt Sally had already cooked enough to fill the refrigerator so that we wouldn't have to cook for a week.

"Good-bye, Alice," she said a little tearfully when the taxi came to take them to the airport.

"We didn't exactly die," I said.

"I know. But it's a whole new life now for you and your father."

"We still have the same house, Dad still has the same job. . . ."

She kissed me on the cheek. "Things will be both the same and not the same," she said. "You can count on it."

Uncle Milt just grinned down at me before he kissed my forehead. "And some things will be even better. You can count on that, too," he said.

I wasn't sure just what time Dad and Sylvia would be arriving, and I didn't know whether to have dinner ready for them or not. But I had been home from school only a few minutes that afternoon when the phone rang.

"Alice?" came a voice I thought I remembered but couldn't recognize. "This is Lois. Are they home yet?"

"No," I said.

"Good! I'll be right over," she said, and hung up.

Now what? I wondered. Even if she *had* been Sylvia's roommate in college, I didn't think she should be here when Dad and Sylvia came back from their honeymoon. I wasn't even sure *I* should be here.

Only ten minutes later I heard a horn beep lightly in the driveway. When I went to the door, Lois was getting out of her car. She motioned me to come outside, and when I got down the steps, Lois was opening her trunk. I gasped at the sight of a woman's nude body curled up inside. Then I realized it was a department-store mannequin, and Lois laughed at the look on my face.

"Ha! Gotcha, didn't I?" she said.

"What are you going to *do* with it?" I asked, puzzled.

"I had a brainstorm and wanted to make sure your aunt and uncle had gone. Help me carry this up to your dad's bedroom."

"What?" I asked, delighted to be in on the joke, whatever it was.

"You get the legs, I'll lift the arms, but let's get her inside before your neighbors call the police," Lois said, and up the front steps we went, across the porch, and on inside. The mannequin didn't weigh much at all, but it was awkward as anything to carry.

"What are we *doing*?" I asked, laughing.

"I'll tell you as soon as we get her upstairs," Lois said.

After we had dumped the mannequin on Dad's bed, which Aunt Sally had so carefully made up that morning, I said, "I thought everyone had gone home after the wedding."

"Everyone but me, I guess. I stayed in town to visit an old friend of mine and got this wild idea. When Sylvia and I were in college, we were invited to a fraternity costume party, and Sylvia went as a belly dancer."

"A belly dancer?" I said, trying to imagine it.

"Yep. And while Nancy and I were looking for something in Sylvia's closet yesterday morning, I found a box of old college stuff. When Nancy discovered the belly dancer costume, I had to tell her the whole story. And I thought, wouldn't it be fun to borrow a mannequin from my friend—she's a department-store buyer—dress it in Sylvia's belly dancer costume, and have it reclining on their bed when they get back from the honeymoon?"

"Oh, it would be so *funny*!" I said, clapping my hands.

"So we've got to get this babe dressed before they walk in." Lois reached in her bag and took out a black spangled bra and black panties with a filmy blue-and-silver skirt attached. "You do the bra, and I'll try to get the pants and skirt on her."

We laughed all the while we were doing it. I think I twisted the arm wrong, and it seemed to go backward. One leg was definitely backward and had to be reversed.

"Sylvia actually wore all this?" I asked, inspecting the spangled bra. "To a *fraternity* party?"

"She sure did. And every guy there was hitting on her, let me tell you."

"And . . . ?" I asked.

"And that's as far as my story goes. If there's more to it, Sylvia will have to tell you herself."

Every so often we were convulsed with laughter when we couldn't move the mannequin's limbs the way they should go, her sultry eyes watching us, her mouth in a permanent pout.

We finally got the mannequin situated just right, resting seductively on the bed, her legs stretched out, one over the other, her cheek propped up on one hand. I even found some glitter to sprinkle in her navel and between her breasts.

"Done!" said Lois. "Now I've got to get back to North Carolina. You'll have to call and tell me how this went over when they got home. But there's one little problem. *Some*body has to get this mannequin back to the Hecht's store at Montgomery Mall, where my friend works. I don't want you to bother Ben with it, and you don't have your driver's license yet. Can you think of anyone who . . . ?"

"Lester," I said. "The very one."

9

Message from Penny

There's a rule in our house that if we can't be home in time for dinner, we're supposed to call— the dinner hour being anywhere between six and seven. So when six fifteen came and I hadn't heard from Dad and Sylvia, I decided that meant they'd be here for dinner.

I opened the refrigerator and found a pan of beef stew that Aunt Sally had made, some leftover corn bread, and a cherry pie. Suddenly inspired, I put the stew over low heat, made a salad, then set the dining-room table with a linen cloth and napkins and two white candles. I found one of Dad's favorite CDs, something by Schubert, and had it ready on the CD player.

Six thirty came, then six forty-five. I turned off the burner under the stew and put the salad back in the fridge. At seven I went to the door and stared out into the street. Not a car in sight.

I went upstairs to my computer and answered some e-mails. I found one from Eric, my friend in Texas:

> Hey, stranger,
> How's it g-g-going?

He always does that for a joke, just because he stutters.

> Haven't heard from you in a while.
> You run off and get married or
> something?
> CAY

I e-mailed back:

> No, my dad did.
> A.

Eric signs himself *CAY* for *Crazy About You*. That's the way he used to sign e-mail messages to me before I even knew who he was, when he was too shy to introduce himself. I looked at the clock. Seven forty-three.

I called Lester. One of his roommates answered and said he had just walked out, but maybe he could snag him. I waited while the guy gave a loud whistle and called Les's name. There was a long pause, the sound of footsteps on wood stairs. A door slamming. Then Lester's voice:

"Al?"

"How did you know it was me?" I asked.

"Paul said it sounded like a young girl. What's up?"

When would I stop sounding like a "young" girl? I wondered. "I think something's happened," I said.

Lester sighed. "Like what? To whom?"

"Dad and Sylvia."

"Why? Did their heads come back in a trunk?"

"Be *serious*!" I said. "It's almost eight o'clock, and they're still not here and nobody's called."

"When did they *say* they'd be back?"

"Wednesday."

"Just Wednesday? No time?"

"No, but . . ."

"It's still four more hours before Thursday, Al."

"But we've always had this rule, Lester, about calling if we can't make it in time for dinner!"

"This isn't an ordinary day, Al. We're talking 'honeymoon' here. There are probably going to be some new rules. Everything's up for grabs."

"Well, nobody told *me* that! In fact, nobody even told me good-bye! I've got dinner on the stove and a salad in the fridge and the table's set

with linen napkins and candles and everything!
Besides, I'm hungry."

"So call Sylvia on her cell phone and ask if
they'll be home for dinner."

"I forgot to get her number. And even if I knew
it, I'm not sure I'd—"

"Okay, Al. Listen to me and do exactly what I say."

I got a pencil ready to write down the number
of the state police and all the hospitals between
here and West Virginia. "Okay," I said.

"Number one," said Lester. "Go to the kitchen.
Two: Put some dinner on a plate. Three: Eat it.
Four: Brush your teeth. Five: Go to bed. Got it?"

"Les-ter!" I wailed. "You're not helping. You
don't know how much work I did to make things
nice for them, and they don't even bother to call."

"Well, nobody told *them* you would have dinner
waiting, and suddenly you've got linen napkins
and candles and a pout the size of Texas on your
face. I've got to go now."

"Lester?"

"*What?*" He sounded in a hurry.

"Will you do a favor for me and take something
back to Hecht's in a couple of days?"

"Sure. I'll pick it up sometime. See ya," he said.

It was a quarter of nine and I was upstairs when I
heard a car door slam. I'd already eaten and put

the rest of the food away. I went to the top of the stairs and watched as Dad and Sylvia came in and set their bags on the floor. Dad saw me at the top of the stairs.

"Al!" he said, breaking into a smile, his arms outstretched, and suddenly I flew down the stairs and gave him a bear hug as he swung me around. I hugged Sylvia, too.

"Did you have a good time?" I asked, then wondered if that was an appropriate question about a honeymoon.

"A *wonderful* time!" Sylvia answered. "And the leaves are absolutely spectacular. It's so gorgeous in West Virginia! I don't see why people feel they have to go to Vermont to see fall colors." She had on a pair of slacks and a suede jacket, loafers on her feet.

"I didn't get a chance to talk with you before we left," Dad said. "How did things go here?"

He didn't even apologize, but I was determined to stay cheerful. "Liz and Pamela stayed over the weekend, and Aunt Sally cooked up a storm." I turned to Sylvia. "The bracelet you left for me is beautiful. Thank you."

"Thank *you*!" she said, turning on a lamp in the living room. Then she saw the dining-room table set with linen and candles. "Oh, Alice! Was this for us?"

Dad looked around and saw the place settings. "You weren't expecting us for dinner, were you, Al?"

"Well, I just thought maybe you'd want something. I wasn't sure when you'd be home," I said.

"We got hungry and decided to get a bite on the road," Dad said.

"Why don't we leave the table just like this and eat here tomorrow night?" Sylvia suggested, and suddenly everything seemed "right" again.

"I wish I had your wedding present done, but I don't," I told them. "It's something I'm making myself, and it's taking a lot more time than I thought."

"Those are the best presents, worth waiting for," said Dad. "We'll appreciate it all the more when it's finished."

We sat in the living room talking for an hour or more—how well the wedding went, the beautiful day, the Greenbrier Resort—and then Dad said, "Well, I'd better get our bags up to our room and let you go to bed, Al. We can't keep you up all night."

He turned out the light and went to the front door to lock it. Sylvia picked up the smaller of their bags and started up the stairs. I followed closely behind.

I saw the light go on in Dad's bedroom. There was a gasp, then a shriek from Sylvia.

"Sylvia?" Dad said.

Her laughter rang out over the hall, and I joined in. Dad came hurrying up, staring at us both.

"What's the matter?" he asked, moving toward their bedroom.

"Oh, Ben!" Sylvia laughed. "Lois has been here. I *know* it was Lois!"

Dad stepped through the doorway, and I crowded in behind him. *"What . . . ?"* And then he started to chuckle. "I'll bet you had something to do with this, Al!"

"Lois said it was Sylvia's story to tell, so my lips are sealed." I giggled. "Something about a fraternity party, though, in case you're interested, Dad."

"Oh, that girl! Now, how did she ever find that costume? I'll bet she and Nancy were going through my closets! It was for a fraternity costume party, Ben. Lois went as Cleopatra, as I remember, and boy, were we *hot!*" She winked at me, and we giggled some more.

Dad was still staring. "You went in *that?*"

"Yeah, Dad, and you have a spaz when I just wear my backless dress!" I teased.

Dad raised his eyebrows, smiling at Sylvia. "So what *did* happen at that party? I'm almost afraid to ask."

"Absolutely nothing, sweetheart, except that I was a hit that night. And so was Lois. There was a lot of flirting going on, and I drank two beers. One of the seniors drove us back to our dorm. And I think Lois and I both kissed him on the cheeks at the same time."

"What are we supposed to do with this . . . uh . . . woman in our bedroom?" he asked.

"Don't worry," I told him. "It has to go back to Hecht's, but Lester said he'd take her."

The wedding had been so much fun that I hadn't thought of much else, but once Dad and Sylvia returned from their honeymoon, I slowly came back to Earth. And what I found myself thinking about most was that there were now two girls at school whom I had hurt; I'd wanted to hurt Penny, but not Amy.

I'd tried to make it up to Amy by being extra nice to her, but Penny avoided me and I couldn't blame her. At the same time, I didn't care. It wouldn't have been so bad, I guess, if, when I was inviting people to Dad's wedding, I'd made it clear that I was asking only those friends who had had Miss Summers as a teacher. Instead, I had included Amy, who hadn't even gone to our junior high, and I'd done all this in front of Penny. That really must have hurt. But did she ever stop to think how *I* felt when she took Patrick away from me? And then, to know that she invited him out on Dad's wedding day, when she *knew* I'd invited Patrick!

I was thinking about Penny, I guess, because the newspaper staff was having a Halloween party at Jayne Renaldi's house, and I remembered that the last Halloween party I'd gone to was at Penny's. I hadn't realized then that she liked Patrick. I just remember that she had looked really sexy in black shorts and a pirate's costume, and the guys sure went for her.

Then I had an awful thought. What if she gave another party sometime and invited everyone but *me*? It's one thing not to be invited to a friend's father's wedding, but not to be invited to a party is a lot worse. And of *course* she wouldn't invite me. Why should she? If *she* went around the tables in the cafeteria whispering invitations to people right under my nose, excluding me, I'd be humiliated.

This could go on all through high school, I was thinking. I insult her. She insults me. And the thing was, neither of us was even going out with Patrick! Why were we still feuding? Because she'd really hurt me, I guess, and it still stung.

"I'm going to a party at our new editor's house on Halloween," I told Dad and Sylvia at dinner on Thursday, when we ate in the dining room with candles on the table.

It was only the second night Dad and Sylvia would sleep together in our house, and it made me feel really weird. The night before—the night they'd come back from their honeymoon—was the worst because I was so afraid I'd hear something I shouldn't. It was crazy! Other kids grow up with dads and moms who have sex, and *they* must hear stuff sometimes.

But as late as it had been, I'd gone into my room and turned on my radio so they'd know I couldn't hear anything. And about eleven Dad tapped on my door and asked if I shouldn't be thinking about going to sleep, that he and Sylvia were tired from their drive home. Could I at least turn the music down? he had asked.

But it wasn't just the nights that were awkward. It was everything. As much as I'd wanted Sylvia Summers for my mom, I felt too formal and polite when she was around. I kept saying "Excuse me" for the smallest burp or bump and always wondered if I was remembering to chew with my lips closed. It didn't feel like *our* house anymore.

"Who's the new editor this year?" Dad asked.

"Jayne Renaldi. She lives somewhere near Colesville Road. It's a party for the newspaper staff."

"Sounds like fun," said Sylvia.

I glanced at Sylvia and then at Dad, and I tried

not to smile. "I was thinking I could go in Sylvia's belly dancer costume."

"Oh!" Sylvia said, and Dad's mouth dropped open.

But he collected himself and said, "Over my dead body."

I just laughed. "*She* went to a party dressed like that, and she's still a respectable woman," I told him.

"Wait till you're in college," said Dad, smiling. "And then, if you're ever invited to a fraternity costume party, maybe Sylvia will lend it to you."

I'd been teasing, of course. I wasn't about to show up in a belly dancer costume. Pamela might do it, but I wouldn't. It would be like going out in public in your underwear. I glanced over at Sylvia as she ate her green beans. She must have had a lot more nerve than I do. I noticed that she held her fork in her left hand, the European way. After she'd cut a piece of meat, she didn't put down her knife and transfer her fork to her right hand the way Americans do.

"What time will you want me to drive you over there?" asked Dad.

"You won't have to drive. Tony's going to pick up a bunch of us and bring us back," I said.

"Tony?"

"The sports editor."

"Well, I'm not sure I'm comfortable with that," said Dad.

"*I* won't be comfortable if *you* drive me. I'd be the only one on the newspaper staff who is driven over by her dad," I said.

"Don't worry. I won't come in and embarrass you or anything."

"He'll only wear his clown costume and do a little dance," Sylvia joked, and we smiled, but I wondered if Dad and I were going to quarrel over this in front of Sylvia.

And then I noticed she had a drop of salad dressing above one corner of her mouth. It sat there glistening like a white pearl—beautiful Sylvia Summers with salad dressing above her lip. I couldn't believe it!

She just went right on talking. So did Dad.

"I guess I always dreaded this day," he said.

"Hey, Dad. I've been to Halloween parties before," I said.

"Not in someone else's car," he told me. "Someone your own age."

"Lester lived through it."

"Yeah, that's how I got this," Dad said, and pointed to the gray in his hair. And then he reached over with his napkin and dabbed at Sylvia's lip.

"Splattering, am I?" she said, and took another bite.

Sylvia seemed comfortable with me. How long would it take me to feel that way around her? Ever? Never? It always felt as though we had a guest. As though I had to get out of the bathroom quickly in case she needed it. When I used the toilet, I sprayed deodorizer all over the place and hoped she wouldn't come in for ten minutes. I'd wipe out the tub when I was through so there wouldn't be any hair lying around, and I put my used tampons in a small grocery sack instead of just wrapping them in toilet paper and dropping them in the wastebasket. I'd never been this careful with Dad or Lester.

Maybe no matter how long Sylvia and I lived together, it wouldn't be the same as having a real mother. Maybe you have to grow up with a person to feel that close. But then, how did people ever get married?

"What are you going to wear?" Pamela asked me on the bus going home the next afternoon when I'd told everyone about the Halloween party.

"We're supposed to come in a costume made of newspaper," I said. "I just found out. It was Jayne's idea."

"Entirely of newspaper?" Elizabeth asked.

"We can use tape to hold it together, but that's all," I told them.

Elizabeth thought that over. "What are you going to wear underneath?"

That's Elizabeth. "Newspaper undies, I guess," I said, then laughed. "Underwear not included."

"How about a sarong?" Pamela suggested. "Liz and I could come over early and fix you up."

"*Would* you?" I cried. "I'll be afraid to move in it, almost."

"What if you have to go to the bathroom?" Elizabeth asked.

"The whole thing comes off," I teased. "This is going to be *some* party!"

I had a ton of homework to catch up on over the weekend. When *The Edge* came out that Friday, I saw that Tim, the new assistant editor, had used three of my suggestions that kids had given me for things they would like to learn before they left high school: how to put on eyeliner, how to deal with a teacher who's sarcastic, and how to unhook a girl's bra. Some kids wanted to know how to snowboard, and others asked how to get along with your girlfriend's mother—things like that. Our list was a real hit. I don't know that the faculty was wild about it, but it got a lot of laughs from our friends.

I didn't have any other newspaper assignments for a while, so that was a relief. But I was beginning to be embarrassed because it was taking so long to finish Dad and Sylvia's wedding present. One of the pillowcases was really wrinkled and soiled, and I had to take some of the stitching out and do it over. I also was helping Dad and Sylvia open the pile of wedding presents we had brought home from the wedding that they hadn't even seen yet. I kept a list of people who were to receive thank-you notes.

I guess I was just feeling sort of . . . well . . . unsettled. I didn't feel I quite knew my place in the family anymore. In fact, sometimes it felt as though I didn't *have* a place. I was so used to being the only female, and suddenly here was Sylvia with clothes to press and presents to open and nails to polish and bras to wash. It was all the more difficult because Les wasn't around. For about as long as I could remember, our family had consisted of Dad and Lester and me. And now it was Dad and Sylvia and me. It wasn't the same at all.

At school on Monday, I was standing in line in the cafeteria. Penny was ahead of Elizabeth, Elizabeth was ahead of me, and I was ahead of Pamela. I kept staring past Elizabeth at Penny, wondering if she had gone out with Patrick Saturday, wondering if that's why he left the reception early, and hating her for trying to ruin Dad's wedding day for me. There was a large platter of fresh fruit on the salad counter, and I think all four of us were eyeing a large ring of pineapple—the *only* piece of fresh pineapple—right in the center, surrounded by melon slices.

Penny reached for the tongs and took the pineapple.

"That's right, take the best one!" Elizabeth kidded.

And before I could stop myself, I heard my own voice saying, "Oh, she's good at that."

To which Pamela added, "Not just pineapple, either."

I think I surprised even Elizabeth. I *know* I surprised myself. It was like I couldn't trust my mouth anymore. I sounded so bitter and petty and quarrelsome that I was embarrassed. It was almost as though the words had to come out—as though they had been trapped in my chest so long, they just exploded from my mouth.

Penny didn't respond to either me or Pamela, though I know she'd heard us. She just said to Elizabeth, "Now, you know that if I hadn't taken it, you would have. Want half?"

"No, that's okay," said Elizabeth, helping herself to the melon. "I like honeydew."

We didn't talk about what I'd said just then or what Pamela had said after I did. What was the matter with me? I wondered. I'd never had a real enemy, unless you counted the Terrible Triplets, as

I called them, back in third grade—three girls who had made my life miserable until they got to know me better—and Denise Whitlock, in seventh, who terrorized me until I got to know *her* better.

The problem with hating Penny was that I had liked her until she stole Patrick from me. Everyone liked her. Everyone still does, probably, except that she committed the unpardonable sin of stealing somebody's boyfriend. But now I found myself avoiding her as she avoided me, averting my eyes if she looked my way.

I helped Sylvia with the dishes after dinner and told her about the newspaper costume I had to wear.

"What fun!" she said. "Now, that's going to take some creativity!"

I spent the rest of Monday evening answering e-mail, and at the bottom of the list I recognized Penny's e-mail address.

My heart began to race. I was almost afraid to open it. Finally I pressed READ.

> How much longer are you going to stay
> mad at me?

My first impulse was to type, *Forever.* Then I stopped. I would think for a long while before answering.

10

Pretending

Penny probably got a ride the next morning because I didn't see her on the bus. Once at school, we both kept our distance, probably trying to figure out what to say to each other. I was glad when the day was over at last and I was home again.

Sylvia must not have heard me come in, because she was taking a nap on the couch. She was dressed in jeans and a yellow T-shirt, with both hands resting on her stomach, and she was snoring. *Snoring!* Not real loud, but loud enough for it to be considered a snore.

I couldn't help myself. I just stood in the doorway staring at her. Beautiful women were just like the rest of us. Their bodies worked exactly the same! I tiptoed on up to my room to study for a sociology test.

A half hour later Sylvia came upstairs.

"I'll bet I was sound asleep and you walked right by me," she said. Her hair was tousled and she still looked sleepy.

"You looked like you could use some sleep." I smiled.

"Well, I'd better not get used to afternoon naps, because I've only got one more week to get myself organized," she said. She came over and handed me a notepad. "I got a call this morning from Lois's friend at Hecht's. She said you should return the mannequin to the Customer Service Department."

"Okay. I'll call Lester," I said.

He wasn't in, but I left a message, asking if he could come by that evening to return something for me to Montgomery Mall.

I know how Lester feels about shopping malls, though. I know how he feels about department stores and especially how he feels about the women's stuff in department stores. So I decided not to even tell him it was a mannequin. I found the long blue tissue-paper bag that Sylvia's wedding dress came in—she'd put it in the trash—and I managed to slip it over the mannequin's head. We had put the mannequin on Lester's old bed, and I carefully wriggled the bag over the shoulders, the hips, the legs, and I stapled the open end. *Perfecto!*

Lester showed up at the house around eight. Dad and Sylvia were out with friends.

"Helloooo!" he called, coming inside.

"It's up here, Les," I said.

He came upstairs and studied the long blue bundle. "What is it?"

"Just a prop Lois borrowed for the wedding. Nothing breakable. I'll help you carry it to the car," I said.

I picked up the end with the head and Lester picked up the bottom. "This isn't heavy," he said. "I can carry it." And before I could protest, he draped the bundle over his shoulder, took it outside, and stuffed it in his trunk. I held my breath.

"So how's it going with Sylvia?" he asked after I got into the car beside him and we headed toward the corner.

"Well," I said, "I just found out she snores."

Lester glanced over at me. "You're monitoring their bedroom now?"

"No. Of course not. She was taking a nap on the couch. Lester, I wish you were still at home. It would be so much easier."

"Two people listening to her snore?"

"I just don't know how to act around her."

"Why are you bothering to act at all? Sylvia lies down and snores, and *she* doesn't care. Why do *your* shorts get all twisted when *she's* around?"

"I don't know. I just don't feel comfortable with

her yet, and I wouldn't feel so weird about things if you were here."

"Weird? You want weird, try having *three* people all wanting to use the bathroom at the same time."

We got to the store about a half hour before closing time.

"So where do we take this thing?" Lester asked.

"Customer Service."

"What entrance?"

"I don't know."

"What floor?"

"I . . . I don't know that, either."

"You don't know what entrance? You don't know which floor?"

"All the note said was Customer Service, Lester. I don't know this store."

I think he swore under his breath. His lips moved, anyway. We both got out of the car, and Les opened the trunk. He grabbed hold of the bundle, and the tissue paper tore. The mannequin's left hand fell out. Lester leaped backward and stared. "Ho-ly . . . !"

I didn't want him to say no now. "It's just a mannequin, Lester. Lois borrowed it as a joke."

"Tell me this," said Lester. "Is she dressed?"

"No," I said.

He gave me a look that could wither plants, then pulled the mannequin out and held one end while he tried to juggle the key to the trunk. The tissue paper gave again, and one of the mannequin's legs slid out.

A middle-aged couple was walking toward us, and I saw the woman suddenly stop and grab the man's arm.

"Put her back," Les said quickly. We stuffed her back inside the trunk and closed the lid till the couple passed by, turning once to look at us. Then we tried again.

"You take one end, I'll take the other, and we'll carry her like we were carrying a rug," said Lester. We started off again, walking sideways toward the entrance.

Somehow this seemed to make it look worse. It's hard to disguise a woman's body, and the tissue paper was a bad idea. Body parts were sticking out all over the place. Three girls and a man passed us, and I saw the girls stop and stare. One of them gave a little shriek. The mannequin's left arm had slipped down and was dragging along the concrete. Les grabbed it up again and placed it on top of the bundle where he could hold on to it.

A lady saw us coming and held the door open for us, then gasped as we went through.

"Customer Service Department?" Les asked a clerk, who pointed to one corner of the store. Customers turned to stare.

It was then that I noticed a blue light flashing outside the glass doors where we had entered, and a moment later a security officer came in.

"Excuse me!" he called, hurrying up behind us as another man, a store detective, obviously, approached from the other direction, cell phone in hand. A small crowd gathered twenty feet away.

Lester looked at me. "You die," he muttered.

"Open the package, please," the store detective said.

"She's naked, sir," Lester told him. The mannequin's arm slid off again, but this time it came completely off, and it was the officer and the detective who saw the plastic joints in the wrist and fingers. They smiled just a little.

"We're returning her to Customer Service," Les said, picking the arm up off the floor.

"Follow me," said the store detective, and as we started off again Lester reached out with the severed arm and bonked me over the head with it.

But when the second arm fell off, Lester handed it to me along with the tissue paper and, tossing the naked lady over his shoulder, followed the detective. I trailed behind, carrying both arms in my hands like baseball bats. We made our way through the counters of men's khakis and chinos.

"She just had a little too much to drink," Lester told one customer who gaped at us open-mouthed. And to another he said, "She's always losing things, this lady. First her clothes, then her arms. . . ." By the time we got to Customer Service, he even had the store detective laughing.

"We've been expecting her," said the woman at Customer Service, smiling. "I hope you gave her a good time!"

On the way home Lester said, "I hope you've had your jollies for the day. Why didn't you *tell* me what it was? We could at least have stuffed her in a garment bag or something. But *tissue paper?*"

"It was the only thing I could think of that would cover her," I said.

"A paper brain, that's what you've got," said Lester. "So what were you and Lois doing with it, anyway?"

I told him then about Sylvia's belly dancer costume and the fraternity party, and at least I got him to smile. "Well, if Dad ever has a dull evening, I guess, Sylvia will know how to liven things up," he said.

After he dropped me off at home later, I sat in front of my computer and stared at yesterday's message from Penny:

How much longer are you going to stay
mad at me?

I clicked on REPLY and typed,

> I really don't know.

After I'd sent it, I wondered if I couldn't have thought of something a little more original and witty than that. I was surprised when a few moments later I got an instant message:

> Well, I wish it was soon, because I'm tired of trying to dislike you.

That was really strange. I typed:

> YOU'RE trying to dislike ME? I don't even have to try when it comes to you.

Penny wrote immediately.

> You must really hate me.

Her openness unnerved me.

> Not hate.

Then she wrote:

> Okay. I hurt you, and I'm sorry, because I

really do like you. But it's not as though it was all my fault, you know.

Now *that* made me mad.

No, you were just minding your own business and Patrick suddenly came on to you?

Penny: I'll admit I liked him, but you can't hold that against me. We can't help who we like, can we? And you *want* other girls to like the guy you're with, don't you?

Me: You knew he was going out with me.

Penny: I knew you guys were together, but at first I was just joking around with him, the way I did with the other guys. Maybe I shouldn't have done that.

Me: Duh!

Penny: Well, what would you do if a guy seemed interested in you but he'd been going out with someone else? Turn your back on him?

Me: I sure wouldn't have acted like I was available.

Penny: I wasn't acting like anything. I wasn't going out with anyone, and everybody knew it. Yes, I knew I could have said something to turn Patrick off whenever we joked around, but I didn't. And you got hurt. And then *I* got hurt when Patrick ended it with me.

Me: And that's supposed to make me feel better? Patrick and I had a good thing going. Then you came along, and now it's over. And you're sorry and want to be friends again.

Penny: I guess that's about it.

Me: Forget it. And in case you think I didn't know you invited him out the day of Dad's wedding, I knew.

Penny: Invited him out?

Me: Duh, again.

Penny: I didn't invite him to go anywhere with me. Dad's manager of the Pavilion and gets a free ticket to everything. A group was playing there last Saturday night with Patrick's favorite drummer. I just asked if he wanted the ticket. He said he already had one, that he was going with his dad. I gave the ticket to someone else.

I didn't know what to say after that. For a while neither one of us wrote anything. Then:

Penny: Look. It's been five months already since Patrick and I broke up. If

you wanted him back so bad, why didn't
you go for him? And don't tell me Patrick
doesn't want you back, because anyone
can tell just by looking that he never
stopped liking you.

That really stopped me dead. I didn't know how
to reply. Before I could think of anything to type,
Penny continued:

I've got a suggestion. Let's just *pretend* to
like each other for a few days and see how
it goes. You don't really have to like me.
Let's just act like we're friends again, and
if it doesn't work out, we'll drop it. Okay?

It was so crazy, I said I'd do it.

Okay,

I typed.

It's all an act, but we'll see how it goes.

Penny: Great! Have a good night.

It took more willpower than I thought I had, but
I typed,

You too.

I went down to the kitchen about ten thirty to get some graham crackers. Sylvia was there, eating a muffin.

"Where's Dad?" I asked, as though I was uneasy being alone with her, which I am. Delighted and uneasy both.

"In bed. I wasn't sleepy, so I read awhile."

They had only been married a week, and already they weren't going to bed at the same time? I was sure learning a lot about marriage. About love. About how it's more like life—it *is* life—than the movies.

I sat down across from her, and she said, "I saw you working on your computer. Can you do a lot of your homework that way? I'm so illiterate when it comes to computers."

"Actually, I was having a weird conversation with somebody," I said. And then, because she didn't pry, I told her, "There's this girl at school, Penny, who caused the breakup between Patrick and me and who wants to be friends again."

Sylvia broke the rest of her muffin in pieces, the sleeve of her lavender robe trailing along the edge of the table. "Yeah? What did you say?"

"I told her I didn't really know if we could stop being enemies or not."

She took a bite of muffin. "Well, that's an honest answer."

"But I don't see how I can. Sometimes I feel like I absolutely hate her. She *knew* Patrick and I had been together a long time, and yet—" I stopped suddenly, horrified at the similarity between what Penny had done and the way my dad had moved in on Sylvia and Jim Sorringer. It was okay for my dad, but not for Penny, is that what I was saying? "I guess I don't know how a person ever gets over it," I said.

"It sure can't be easy," Sylvia said, and I wondered if she was thinking the same thing. There were two worlds here, Sylvia's and mine. We could talk about mine, maybe, but I didn't think I could ever ask about hers.

We were both quiet for a few moments while Sylvia went on eating her muffin. After a while she said, "I noticed you and Patrick dancing at the reception. Is he . . . well . . . still in the picture?"

"We're friends," I said. "At least we're back to being that again. But we're not going out or anything. Neither are he and Penny. That's what's so weird. I mean, if I really want him back, why don't I go for it? It's like I can't forgive him either."

"Oh, I don't know. Maybe 'forgiveness' isn't the right word here," Sylvia said. "Maybe you both just need time to back off and see how you feel about each other."

I thought of the way Sylvia Summers had gone to England for a year to try to make up her mind about whom she loved most—Jim Sorringer or Dad. I took a chance. "Maybe I should go to England for a year," I joked.

She looked at me strangely, as though I'd caught her off guard. Then she laughed. "I don't think you have to go *that* far. But what did you decide to do about Penny?"

"We agreed to *pretend* to like each other for a few days and see how it goes," I said.

Her eyes opened wide in surprise. "My gosh! Let me know what happens."

On the bus the next morning Penny called, "Hi, Liz. Hi, Alice," when we got on.

"Hi, Penny," I said, and went to the back to sit with Pamela. She raised one eyebrow at me, looked toward Penny, then back again. I shrugged.

At lunch I forced myself—one foot in front of the other—to carry my tray to the table where Penny was sitting and sit down beside her. I figured at least we wouldn't have to stare at each other every time we looked up if we were side by side.

"What's up?" I said.

The guys didn't seem to notice—well, I saw Patrick look our way—but the girls sure did.

Karen nudged Jill, and I figured she'd have the gossip mill going before lunch period was over.

"Same old," Penny said. "Got a C on that test on the Proterozoic era. There's got to be someone in the universe who can make rocks sound exciting, but this teacher isn't the one."

Pamela kept studying us, wondering what was going on. But Elizabeth is all for reconciliation when possible, and she said, "Alice is going to a Halloween party on Friday—the school newspaper staff—and they all have to come in costumes made out of newspaper."

"What?" said Penny, breaking into a grin.

"How about a newspaper bikini?" said Mark.

"A thong," said Brian.

"I think she should go in a muumuu," said Elizabeth.

"What about a bikini top and a grass skirt made of paper?" said Penny.

"That's it!" said Pamela. "Do that, Alice! That's better than a sarong."

"Yeah, a grass skirt with strips of newspaper for the grass," said Karen.

Well, maybe, I thought. At least I'd be able to sit down without ripping the paper. "Okay, I'll do it!" I said.

The bell rang.

"See you," said Penny.

"See you," I said.

Pamela walked beside me as we left the cafeteria. "Well, *that* was a change," she said. "I thought you two were mortal enemies."

"No, I decided to grow up," I said. For a few days, anyway.

11

Party

The problem was that I thought life would be perfect after my dad married Sylvia Summers. If you had asked me that, I would have said of course not, nothing is perfect, but still, in my heart . . .

The second week after the wedding, for example, I swung back and forth between loving to see Sylvia puttering around our kitchen and resenting the fact that she was in our bathroom when I needed it.

One of the things I like about her is that she's sort of funky in the mornings. She speaks in monosyllables. Dad might say, "I'm making an omelet, Sylvia. Want one?" And she'll just say, "Toast," with her eyes half closed. Or Dad will tell her he's going in early and he'll go over his whole schedule for the day. When he's through, his hand on the door, she'll just say, "Bye."

She says it's because she's lived alone for so long

that she doesn't know how to act in civilized society between six and eight in the mornings. Sometimes, when she's trying to read the paper during breakfast, she looks a little cross-eyed, like her eyes aren't in focus. Dad thinks it's funny. She reminds us of Lester that way. He's not a morning person either.

So much of the time, though, it was like I was waiting for a guest to go home, yet this *was* her home. She had put her house on Saul Road up for sale and was slowly moving her things here. Two new chairs in our living room, a teak buffet in the dining room, lamps, a couple of bookcases and end tables. Our house was looking very nice— comfortable and cozy.

But I would probably never have my dad to myself again, I thought. No long conversations at the table without Sylvia there in the background. Why was I feeling this way? What was wrong with me? I wondered. Dad and Sylvia seemed perfectly content. Yet here I was in this house with a woman I'd always known as a teacher, and I was afraid I'd do something to embarrass either her or myself. I was afraid to be me.

Lester wasn't living here anymore, a girl I'd hated was being nice to me, Algebra II was even harder than I'd thought, and so far Dad's marrying Sylvia hadn't changed any of these things. I got

Sylvia for a stepmom, and I still had all the problems I had before, plus some new ones.

As for Sylvia herself, she wasn't always the glamorous person she was at school, and this really surprised me. When she first got up, her hair was a mess, her face was pale, and she was so long-waisted, I discovered, that her body seemed unnaturally stretched between her neck and waistline. I guess I couldn't get over the fact that she was a living, breathing person who had the same bodily functions I did. And that Dad loved her even when she looked like she had a headache and toothache, both at the same time.

I decided that I would feel a lot better if I could just finish embroidering those stupid monograms, give them the present, and get it over with. I had made such a mess of one of the doves that I had to start again. *A half hour each night until you finish,* I told myself.

Pamela and Elizabeth came over Friday night to help me make my costume for the Halloween party.

Pamela took my bikini bathing suit top and prepared to cover it with newspaper. "What do you want over your breasts?" she asked. "The comics, the business section, or the food section?"

"Give her the food," said Elizabeth, grinning, "in case some of the guys get hungry."

I swatted at her, and we all took sections of the newspaper and began. Elizabeth cut out long strips of newspaper for the skirt, and I went to work covering a belt with stock market quotes. We'd attach the strips to that. It was amazing how many overlapping strips it took to make me look decent. I was going to wear a pair of black spandex running shorts underneath.

"Okay, we're ready, Alice," Elizabeth said. "If you have to go to the bathroom, go now."

Pamela had not only covered the bikini bra with newspaper, but she'd let five-inch strips of paper dangle down all around it, like a fringe, so that it looked more like a loose top.

"Wow!" said Elizabeth when I was dressed.

Even before I got to the mirror, I could hear the newspaper rustle with each step. And there I was, a Hawaiian dancer.

"Wow!" I repeated, staring at myself, the way the paper skirt trembled and swayed with the slightest movement, like rushes in the wind.

"Woo! Shake it, babe!" said Pamela.

"She needs a Hawaiian lei," said Elizabeth, crumpling pieces of the comic section into flowers, to be strung on a thread.

"And a flower behind her ear," Pamela decided. "Man, Patrick should see you now!"

"Why Patrick?" I asked.

"*All* the guys should see you!" said Elizabeth. "Who's driving you to the party, Alice? One of the seniors? You'd better watch you don't get attacked in that outfit."

"Don't worry, I'll take an anti-rape pill," I joked.

Elizabeth stopped stringing flowers together and stared at me. "There's an anti-rape pill?" One thing Elizabeth and Aunt Sally have in common: Their sense of humor isn't very developed.

"Sure," said Pamela, without cracking a smile. "You take one of these pills before you go on a date, and if a guy tries something you don't like, your blood pressure rises and this activates the pill, which makes you give off this really foul odor, and he's instantly repelled."

"What?" said Elizabeth, her eyes widening. "Really?"

"You've never heard of them?" I said. "Liz, where have you *been*?"

"So *tell* me!" she begged.

"Well, the odor starts at the lips, the instructions say, so that your breath is horrendous, and then it travels on down your body. It comes from your nipples next, and if the guy keeps going and tries to get your pants off, the odor will almost knock him out."

"What *is* it? What's it called?" Elizabeth asked.

Pamela and I exchanged glances.

"I think it's called S-T-O-P," Pam said. And suddenly we couldn't help ourselves; Pamela and I doubled over with laughter. Then Elizabeth started to laugh.

"I swear, Liz, you'll believe anything," said Pamela.

Shortly after Pamela and Elizabeth went home, I came downstairs to wait for Tony. Dad had finally agreed to let me ride to the dance with him as long as he came inside first and they met. He wasn't just going to sit out on the driveway and honk, Dad said. I'd told Tony that at school.

"Whatever," he'd said. I didn't think that *whatever* would get him any points from my dad.

Sylvia gasped and clapped when she saw me. "Oh, I've just got to get a picture of this!" she said, and went for her camera.

"I assume there's more underneath that skirt than meets the eye?" Dad said.

"Not to worry," I told him, whirling around so he could see how well my paper skirt worked with the spandex shorts.

I heard Tony's car drive up and went to the door to meet him. I could hear laughter coming from the car, so I knew he'd picked up some of the others first.

"Hi," I said as he came up the steps. I don't

know who made his costume, but he looked like the king of Siam in full newspaper pants gathered at the ankles. "Wow! Look at you!"

"Heeeey!" he said. "Look at *you!*" I led him inside.

"Dad, this is Tony," I said.

"Hello," said Dad, putting down his magazine.

"How you doin'?" Tony said.

Dad smiled as he studied Tony's costume. "Something out of *Arabian Nights?*"

"King of Siam, I think," I told him.

"My sisters made it for me, actually," said Tony.

"Any idea what time this party will be over, Tony?" Dad asked.

"Haven't the faintest," Tony said. Sylvia came to the doorway just then and took a picture of the two of us.

"Sylvia, this is Tony Osler. Tony, my new step-mom," I said.

"Hi," said Tony.

"I'll get an extra print for you if the picture turns out," Sylvia told him.

"How far away is it you're driving?" Dad asked Tony.

"Couple miles. Jayne's on the other side of Silver Spring."

"Well, I'd like the assurance that there won't be any stopping on the way home when the party's over. And it goes without saying that I expect you to stay drug- and alcohol-free," Dad said as I cringed. Then he added, a twinkle in his eye, "And, of course, you will keep yourself physically strong, mentally awake, morally straight, and obey the Scout law."

Tony put up his hands as if in surrender. "Hey, what kind of a party do you think this is?" he said, laughing a little. "Our adviser's going to be there too, you know."

"Glad to hear it," Dad said. "Have a good time, then. And, Al, if you ever need to call home, just do it. I don't care if it's the middle of the night."

"Okay, Dad. Bye," I said, almost stumbling over my feet to get away. I grabbed my jacket from the closet. "Bye, Sylvia."

When we got outside, Tony said, "Man, is *he* something else!"

"Yep! That's my dad!" I said.

Sam Mayer was in the car along with one of the junior roving reporters. I couldn't tell what their costumes were, but there was a constant rustling of paper from the four of us—just breathing made it rustle—and that got us laughing.

I wasn't the only one at the party in a grass skirt. In fact, Jayne was wearing one too, and so was one of the guys, complete with a black wig with a flower in it. Miss Ames, our adviser, came in a long gown made from want-ad sections, and half the fun was watching someone's costume rip. Jayne's dad took pictures of us singly, then as a group. I noticed the way Jayne and her mom laughed together as they put out the food, shared a secret passing through a doorway, caught each other's eye sometimes, and laughed at a joke. I wondered if Sylvia and I would ever be like that. I was too afraid that whatever closeness we felt would be too much like pretending—too much like what it was between Penny and me.

After all, you can't just suddenly feel close to somebody. As much as I loved Sylvia, she still didn't seem like a relative. Somewhere I read that a newborn calf can tell its mother from all the other cattle just by her smell and the sound of her moo. And I suppose human babies, from the time they're born, are familiar with their mothers' voices and smells and touch and feel. I never had that with Sylvia. I never knew what it was like to snuggle against her when I was hurt or scared. And I was afraid that no matter how much I had wanted her for a mom, I would never be that close to her.

But the party was fun. The guys kidded around, trying to read an article on my bra top, turning me this way and that.

"Watch it!" I said, playfully slapping Sam when

he tried to read *under* the fringe of my top, and he just caught my fingers and grinned at me.

"So how's it going?" he asked at some point during the evening.

"What's 'it'?" I said.

"Oh, life in general. Your love life in particular," said Sam, smiling.

I laughed. "How's *yours*?"

He shrugged. "Jen and I broke up, you know."

"Yeah, I heard," I said.

"And so did you and Patrick."

"Yeah, I heard that, too," I said, and smiled back.

The doorbell kept ringing all evening as trick-or-treaters came to the house, but it usually ended with the kids craning their necks to see all the people inside dressed up in newspaper.

We danced later. Jayne taught us a dance called the Fish, which is about the silliest dance I'd ever seen, in which we shaped bubble rings coming out of our mouths with our fingers and waved our rear ends from side to side like fish swimming upstream. Everyone danced together so we didn't need partners, and I thought how nice it is sometimes to just be part of a group, not a couple.

We ended the evening trying to melt candy corn over a candle and mixing it with a Milky Way bar to see what it would taste like (pretty good, actually), but Jayne's mom was afraid we'd set our costumes on fire, so she snuffed the candle out. I wasn't the only one with a protective parent.

"We've got a good start this year, gang," Miss Ames said as we were getting ready to leave. "We had a great response to the article on what students would like to learn before they graduate, and that means *The Edge* is relevant. We need more articles like this, so keep the ideas coming."

Tony drove us home then. He didn't drink and he wasn't on drugs, but I was a little uneasy when he took the other kids home first, though he'd picked me up last. But all he wanted to do, it seemed, was talk.

"You going to get your driver's license soon?" he asked.

"As soon as I can," I told him.

"When's your birthday?"

"May."

"Do it! It's like you're suddenly free, you know? You've got wings. You can go almost anyplace you want."

"Great! I'll head for Miami Beach," I joked. "Is this your own car?"

"Yep. Dad said if I passed my driver's test, I'd get a car."

I glanced over at Tony. "That's all you had to do? Get your license and he bought you a car?"

"Yeah, but if I have an accident, I'll have to start

paying for my own insurance, so I drive careful. It's a used car, of course. A demo. We got a good deal on it."

"Yeah, it's nice," I said, though I can't tell one car from another. If a guy thinks I'm going to be impressed by his car, he's going to be disappointed. Things seem to come so easily for some people, I was thinking. I would never in a million years expect my dad to buy a car for me just because I passed my driver's test and got a license.

Tony talked about his dad then—the kind of work he did and how he was so busy that Tony didn't see much of him. He told me that his family used to live in Massachusetts before his dad got transferred here and that he himself had a genetic heart defect so he couldn't play football, but at least he'd made sports editor for the newspaper. . . .

And then we were turning in the driveway at my house, and he said good night and that was it. All he'd wanted, it seemed, was someone to listen to him talk, mostly about himself. I didn't know whether to feel insulted or flattered. Flattered, I decided, because I suppose that shows I'm a person people feel comfortable talking with.

But if I'm a person people can talk to so easily, why couldn't I feel more comfortable talking with Sylvia? Why couldn't I come to breakfast in an old mangy bathrobe without brushing my teeth and hair and ask if she'd ever had bad cramps? *She* comes to breakfast half asleep sometimes. Why couldn't I ask her how to do my hair in a French braid? Ask her to rub my back or whether she'd like me to rub hers?

Is that the way mothers and daughters talked to each other? I wondered. I didn't know. I had a mom now, and half the time I couldn't even think what to say.

Dad and Sylvia were still up. Dad was sitting at one end of the couch, and Sylvia was lying down, her head at the other end, her legs over Dad's lap. He was caressing her feet. I sat down and told them all about the party.

"Aren't you freezing?" Dad asked.

"Now that I think about it, yes. Guess I'll get in the tub," I said, and went upstairs so they could enjoy their "quality time."

I figured it was too late to call Pamela and Elizabeth and tell them about the party, but after I'd had my bath, I checked my e-mail. There was a message from Penny:

> So how did it go, the grass skirt? I'll bet
> you were hot!

I e-mailed back:

> It was fab. I'll show you the pictures
> when I get them.

It was almost easier talking to Penny than it was to Sylvia.

12

Tooth Troubles

Now that the wedding was over, I felt I couldn't wait any longer to tell Dad about my visit to the dentist a few months back. I knew that braces were expensive, and this on top of the wedding. . . . Could Dad even afford the remodeling if we had to wire my mouth?

"Dad," I said on Sunday morning when he and Sylvia were having coffee. By nine o'clock on weekend mornings Sylvia's usually talking in sentences. "You know when I went to the dentist after I came home from camp? Well, I didn't want you to worry about this until after the wedding, but he thinks I need braces. He says I should see an orthodontist."

"Oh?" said Dad. "Why?"

"I'm not sure. I forget exactly. Something about my bite."

Lester had come in the back door while I was

talking. He often drops in on Sundays when he knows Dad will be home. Frankly, I think he misses us. I asked him once which he missed most: me or Dad's pancakes. And he said, "Pecan or plain?"

Now he poured himself a cup of coffee and said, "Did I hear someone say 'braces'?"

"Me," I said mournfully.

Lester leaned against the counter and studied me.

"Underbite?" he asked. "Do this." He thrust out his lower jaw.

I thrust out my jaw while he examined me.

"Hmm," said Lester. "Overbite? Do this." He pulled back his lower lip so that his upper teeth stuck out over the lower. I did what he said.

"Now," said Lester, "say 'Freddy fries five flavorful fish' six times, as fast as you can."

"Les-ter!" I said. "Can't you be serious when my whole high school career is in jeopardy?"

Lester dramatically clutched his heart.

"Did the dentist say how long you might need to wear them?" asked Sylvia, looking unkempt but natural in a brown-and-yellow silk robe.

"About two years," I said, and immediately felt tears well up in my eyes. Why do they *do* that? When will I stop crying every time there's a problem in my life? What will I do when something *really* serious happens? Explode? But I was beyond

reason. "Two years out of the best years of my life!"
I wept. "Two years looking like I've got a razor wire
fence in my mouth. No boy will want to kiss me.
Boys won't even want to get near me!"

"Good," said Dad. "I feel better already."

"Ben," said Sylvia, chiding. And then she said,
"I used to wear braces."

I stopped whimpering. "You did?"

"I was a little younger than you are now, but my
overbite needed correcting. If it's boys you're worried about, look at me: I married the man of my
dreams."

Dad had a banana-shaped smile on his face.

"If you really need them, Al, then of course
you'll get braces. We'll make the appointment,
and I'll go with you," he said.

Sylvia reached over and put her arm around me.
"Think positive. Who knows? The next two years
of your life could be wonderful."

Yeah, right, I thought.

Dad doesn't fool around. The next week I was
sitting in the orthodontist's chair, watching the
plastic model of human teeth open and close in
the doctor's hand. He was standing beside my
chair explaining my problem to Dad. He moved
the bottom teeth forward until they evenly
matched the top teeth. Then he overlapped the

top teeth so they stuck out over the ones below. He pointed to the incisors at the sides of the dental plates. He pointed to the gums behind the two rows of teeth, where the wisdom teeth were poking through.

At some point he put the plastic model back on the tray and turned to Dad again, using his hands to explain something.

I picked up the teeth, squeezed the sides, and watched them open and close on their hinges. When the jaws snapped together, the teeth were firmly locked in place. I couldn't help myself. I squeezed the plastic teeth open and gently clipped them to the bottom of Dr. Wiley's white coat. I saw Dad's eyebrows rise, then come together over the bridge of his nose as Dr. Wiley kept right on talking and gesturing. Dad was trying not to laugh, I could tell.

Dr. Wiley swung around then, and the teeth clunked against my chair. He reached down and found the plastic teeth clamped to the hem of his jacket. He looked at me and laughed. I figured that any man who could laugh at teeth hanging over his rear end at least had a sense of humor.

"All you need to decide now, Alice, is what color beads you would like on your braces," he said. "That's all the rage. You don't fight your braces, you flaunt them!"

I was about to choose green, but then I figured it would always look as though I had lettuce stuck in my teeth. But if I chose pale pink and blue, my mouth would look like a baby's crib. "No colors," I said. "Just stick to silver, please." Then I settled back to let him make an impression of my teeth and do the preliminary work.

You know what I was worrying about? Not so much the pain, which most of my friends had said was bearable. Not even the fact that food would get stuck in my braces and everyone would know it but me. I think I was scared that on some level I was going to be left behind by my friends. Most of the girls who got braces in middle school had them off by now. All the jokes and embarrassments and agonies were passé, and the kids I hung out with had moved on to more sophisticated topics. And here I would come, with my sore gums and wires and metallic smile, like the girl who doesn't get her period till she's seventeen.

Guys might think of asking me to the Snow Ball and then remember The Mouth. Girls might get together for pizza but wouldn't invite me because they weren't sure what I could eat. I hadn't even got the wires on yet, and already I had excluded myself from half the human race.

That night I e-mailed Eric in Texas.

You think you've got problems? I'm going
to have a mouthful of metal soon. Braces!
Ugh!

Back came an e-mail from Eric:

Too bad I don't have braces. Then I could
blame all my s-s-stuttering on that.

I answered:

Does it still bother you much? Stuttering?

And Eric replied:

No, especially since I met a girl named
Emily. I guess I should tell you that she's
really special.

Oh, man, I was even losing Eric! I thought
awhile before I answered. Did I care? I guess I
did, in a way. Not that I wanted Eric to pine away
for me down in Texas when we might not ever
see each other again. I guess I just missed being
special to someone. Missed being the only female
in the family. Missed having Lester around all the
time to pay attention to me. Was already missing
the me who wasn't afraid to smile.

That's wonderful, Eric. Eric and Emily!
Sounds good together!

I lied.

It helped a little now that Sylvia was teaching
again. We were on more of a schedule. I knew
when she'd be getting up in the mornings and
what time she left for school. She was usually out
of the bathroom before I'd finished breakfast, and
I learned to blow-dry my hair in my own room,
freeing the bathroom for Dad.

Hard as it was to get used to Sylvia in our
house, I wondered how it was for her. Here we
were, a settled household, and somehow she had
to find a way to fit in. If it were *me* moving into
her house and her routine back on Saul Road,
would it have been easy for me? I don't think so.

We each had our night to cook. Dad did the
cooking on Sundays, I was responsible for
Tuesdays and Thursdays, and Sylvia did the rest.
At least having scheduled duties made us feel
more like a family, I think. But it was still easier to
talk to Sylvia about my friends than to talk about
myself. It was a start, though, and now I looked for
a chance to find her alone *without* Dad around.
When he came home after work, it seemed he
could hardly wait to put his arms around her. They

liked to tell each other every little detail of what had gone on in their lives that day. I'd sit in the next room doing my homework and think how fascinated they were with each other. When you're in love, you want to share every single thing, I guess.

Dad works late on Thursday evenings, and on this particular Thursday, a week before Thanksgiving, Sylvia and I had dinner together—a chicken and pasta dish with artichokes and black olives. It was a recipe I'd copied from a woman who used to cook for us when I was in fourth grade, Mrs. Nolinstock.

"What do you do," I asked Sylvia, "when there's a girl who really needs a friend and you just don't want to be that chummy with her? I mean, I feel sorry for Amy and I try not to be mean or anything, but I don't especially want to do things with her either."

Sylvia pierced a black olive with her fork and put it in her mouth. "You know," she said, "there are some problems that just don't have a good solution."

"I feel so guilty," I went on. "She's obviously lonely, and some of the other kids . . . okay, *we* . . . laugh at her sometimes. She comes out with the stupidest remarks—meaningless stuff—and she doesn't even seem to notice." I smushed an arti-

choke and swirled it around on my plate. "But she looks so pathetic, and then I feel horrible."

Sylvia nodded. "Oh, I know. I can remember girls like that back in high school."

"She wants to be part of our group so bad, and nobody wants her, including me."

"It's rough, because you can't *make* yourself like someone, can you?" said Sylvia.

We ate quietly for a minute or two.

"What I'd *like* to do sometimes is just shake her and point out how stupid she sounds when she says the first thing that comes into her head," I said.

"Is there some way you could let her know privately when she says something like that? Better she hears it from someone who's kind," said Sylvia.

"I suppose."

"I'm not saying this will happen with Amy," Sylvia went on, "but sometimes, after a while, we find something about a person we really like. That helps us overlook the other stuff."

It was possible, I guess. I don't think I'd especially liked Elizabeth or Pamela when I first met them, either, and now they're like sisters to me. At least *Penny* and I were on speaking terms again. I knew it would be a long time, maybe never, before I felt close to her, but at least we talked and joked around a little.

* * *

Dad and Sylvia and I were going out to dinner on Thanksgiving because Lester was spending the day with friends.

I got my braces the day before, and I sat in the orthodontist's chair plotting murder for every person who had told me it "wasn't too bad." Okay, it wasn't like catching your hand in the car door or having a dentist drill without Novocain, but just when I'd think the orthodontist couldn't make the wires any tighter, he'd tighten them some more. If it hadn't been for the lip spreader, I would have bitten off his fingers.

When he was through and asked me how I was doing, I just grunted at him. I had to come back in a week so he could torture me all over again? He gave me a list of foods I should avoid— nothing hard, sticky, chewy, nothing with a peel or kernels—and I took the bus home, huddled against a window, looking out at all the normal people who could still chew. The last thing in the world you want to do when you get your braces is eat, and the next-to-last thing you want to do is smile. The spacers the orthodontist put in my mouth to make room for the band installation felt like meat permanently stuck in my mouth. I felt as though I had rocks on my teeth. All I wanted to do when I got home was drink a milk

shake and go to bed, but my mouth was so sore
that I couldn't sleep.

It didn't feel much better the next morning,
so I finally took a pain reliever. Amazing what a
little relief will do. I realized I was ravenously
hungry.

"Think you can manage to go out for dinner?"
Dad asked me. "We're skipping the turkey this
year. We figured we'd go for Italian. Soft ravioli
might go down pretty well."

It did. We went, I ate, and I even smiled a time
or two. Nobody even missed the Thanksgiving
turkey. Another tradition, like the throwing of the
bridal bouquet, that we didn't *have* to follow, and
the world didn't end.

On Saturday, Pamela and I spent the night at
Elizabeth's and played "bear and bunny" with her
little brother, Nathan, his favorite game. He covers
a card table with a blanket to make his "cave," and
every time he comes out, the three of us crawl
around on our hands and knees, growling like
bears, and try to catch him. He goes absolutely
bananas.

Nathan found my braces fascinating. He kept
wanting to touch them and would try to pry my
lips open, making us all laugh, when I held him
on my lap.

"You know, Alice," Pamela said, "you *can* smile with your lips apart occasionally. We all know you have braces. It's not as though you have a mouthful of rotting teeth."

I flashed the widest smile I could manage, and she pretended to be blinded by the glare. I realized that as long as I didn't bore people by continually talking about them, braces weren't going to make that big a difference, and I *wasn't* going to be left behind.

Later, when Nathan had gone for his bath and the three of us were sprawled on Elizabeth's twin beds in exhaustion, Liz asked, "What about taking dinner to Lester and his roommates next week?"

"Yes! Let's *do* it!" said Pamela. "Which night?"

"Friday," I suggested, remembering that Les had often hung around our house on Fridays, tired from work or school, and had saved his Saturdays for dating. "If any of them do go out, it'll probably be late in the evening, because they're tired when they first come home. I'll bet we'd find them all in if we went over around seven or seven thirty. After nine, I don't know."

"All right! What will we make?" asked Elizabeth.

I thought a moment. "Lasagna? Why don't you and I make the lasagna, Liz, and Pamela can bring the salad. I'll make a pineapple upside-down cake for dessert."

It was something to look forward to.

"How are we going to get over there?" asked Elizabeth. We frowned for a moment, considering.

Then Pamela said, "I suppose I *could* ask Mom to drive us. She's been after me to let her back into my life. This way we can include her without my having to talk to her for very long."

Strange, I thought, how simple conversation could be so difficult for human beings. Penny and me, Sylvia and me, Pamela and her mother, Amy and almost everybody. . . . If we were dogs, we'd just sniff each other and that would be that. It's hard, sometimes, to be human.

"And dress sexy!" Pamela was saying. "We're hoping, of course, that they'll invite us to stay for dinner."

"Of course," I said. "But what if Lester's right and his roommates are covered with warts?"

Pamela grinned. "Then we'll just have to concentrate on Lester, won't we?"

I hated going to school on Monday. I'd told my friends by e-mail that I was getting braces so they wouldn't be shocked when they saw me, but of course they were all waiting to see how I looked.

"Hmm," said Patrick when he saw me. "I see you've added something."

"Yeah," I said. "Lucky me."

"It's not forever," he said. I *knew* they weren't forever. What I wanted him to say was something like, *You're just as pretty as you were before.* But if he had, I'd only think he was lying.

"Hey!" said Brian. "Does she bite?"

I certainly felt like it. It was Amy who said the kindest thing: "Your smile's so nice, Alice, people notice that first off."

"Thanks, Amy," I said. "Just what I needed to hear."

"Liz and Pam and I are getting together tonight," I told Sylvia when she came home from school on Friday. "Liz is coming over to help me cook, and then we're going to spend the night at her house."

"Oh, really? Then I think Ben and I will go out for dinner and see a movie," she said.

I'm not sure why I didn't tell her what I was planning. Probably because she'd tell me that it wasn't a good idea, and I didn't want to hear it.

I made the pineapple upside-down cake while the pasta was boiling, and Elizabeth and I managed to have both the cake and the lasagna done by the time Pamela and her mom drove up at seven thirty. Mrs. Jones was acting sort of like a teenager herself, trying too hard to fit in.

"This is *fun!*" she said. "And the boys don't even know you're coming?"

I hadn't heard Lester referred to as a "boy" for a

long time. Maybe she had forgotten just how old my brother was.

"Yeah. We thought we'd surprise them," I said.

"Well, you just give me a call on my cell phone, and I'll be back later to pick you up," Mrs. Jones said.

She wears jeans so tight that they pull around her thighs. Her jacket was made of soft black leather that looked and felt like butter. Of course, we looked pretty hot ourselves. Pamela had on tight jeans too, and a top that laced across the front. Fortunately, she had a camisole underneath. Liz and I were in our best jeans and shirts and jackets.

Pamela, the salad bowl in her lap, sat up front with her mom. Elizabeth and I sat in back. I had wrapped the hot lasagna dish in a towel and held it on my thighs, while Liz carried the cake.

"Well, Alice, you finally got a mom!" Mrs. Jones said. "How does it feel to have another female around the house?"

Weird, I wanted to say, but it came out, "Wonderful."

"It's nice to have someone to share all your little secrets, isn't it?" Mrs. Jones was talking, of course, about the kind of relationship she wanted with Pamela. Elizabeth looked at me and rolled her eyes.

"Oh, she's got us," Pamela told her mother. "Any secrets Alice has, she tells them to us."

It wasn't the answer Mrs. Jones wanted to hear. She drove a few minutes more in silence, but as we got closer to Takoma Park, she giggled and said, "Do you think I ought to come in and play chaperone? I hope I don't get in trouble now, delivering you girls to the bachelor apartment of three young men."

"Hey, Mom," Pamela said, "Lester's not into incest, you know."

We turned onto Lester's street, and I directed Mrs. Jones to the big yellow house with the wrap-around porch. There seemed to be only one light on in a window on the first floor, but several lights were on above.

"I hope they're all home," I said eagerly. "Thanks, Mrs. Jones."

She pulled up in front. "Well, here we are, then!" she said. "Have fun, but call me if the party gets rough."

"Mom!" said Pamela.

I really think Pam's mother wanted to be invited in too, but we weren't about to do that. We got out, trying not to slam the car door too loudly. Mrs. Jones drove off, and we walked up the path to the side entrance and started up the steps.

I got to the top first and peeked through the

small window in the door. I could hear voices and music from inside.

"As soon as someone opens the door, we all yell 'Surprise!'" Elizabeth reminded us.

I was just about to knock on the door with my knee when I saw a young woman cross the center hall and disappear into the back room where the kitchen was.

"Pamela!" I said. And then another woman crossed the hall in the other direction, holding a wineglass in her hand. "Elizabeth!" I gasped. The three of us, holding our offerings, stared through the window.

"They're having a party!" Pamela said in disappointment.

Now a man appeared, then a third woman in a thin dress.

"They're having an orgy!" Elizabeth cried.

"They are not!" I said.

"That woman's in her slip," said Elizabeth.

"It's not a slip, it's a cocktail dress," said Pamela.

"How do you know it's not a slip? I don't want to walk in on something we're not supposed to see," said Elizabeth.

"I don't want to walk in at all," I said, suddenly embarrassed at my stupidity in thinking this would work. "We'll look like dorks!"

"Maybe we could just set the food out here, knock, and run," Elizabeth said.

"They've got food. Lester's cooking Chinese. I can smell it all the way out here," I said.

"I still think we ought to go ahead with our plan and give it to them," Pamela insisted. "They'd at least be grateful. You can always use more food at a party."

"We'd look like lunatics," I said.

"Yeah, I suppose. Worse yet, they'd ask us to stay for dinner, and we'd sit around looking like virgins," said Pamela.

"We *are* virgins," said Elizabeth. In the light from the window she looked hard at Pamela and me. "Aren't we?"

"We're virgins," I said.

"Let's leave before someone else comes and finds us out here," Elizabeth said.

"I'll call Mom on my cell phone," Pamela muttered.

Hugely disappointed, we went back down the steps, hoping that maybe Mrs. Jones had just cruised the block and was coming back to see if we needed her. We got to the fourth step from the bottom, and standing right next to us on the wraparound porch was an elderly man, his hands in his pockets, looking at us fiercely.

13

Dinner with the CIA

It could only be Mr. Watts, who owned the house. We didn't know whether to run back up or rush on down. We were three girls, all dressed up with no place to go, holding a salad, a lasagna, and a pineapple upside-down cake.

"Hello," I said, feeling the need to say *something*.

At first I didn't think he was going to answer at all. Maybe, like Grandpa McKinley, his mind was sort of slipping and he was confused a lot of the time. He studied us for a moment and then said, "I see you've brought me some dinner. Come on in."

Now it was *our* turn to stare. Pamela and Elizabeth looked at me.

"Smells like lasagna," he said, and motioned us around to the front door.

Otto Watts rents the upstairs apartment free,

except for utilities, to Lester and his two friends as long as one of them is always there in the evenings in case Mr. Watts needs help. They also do odd jobs for him. That was the agreement—a great deal for graduate students, a pretty good arrangement for Mr. Watts, who already has someone look in on him during the day.

"He's safe," I whispered, nudging Pamela to go on down. We followed the path around to the porch steps. Mr. Watts held the door open for us and followed us inside.

His high-ceilinged living room with the velvet drapes looked like something out of a *Masterpiece Theatre* production. Maybe it was because the Victorian living room was so large that Mr. Watts looked so small, but he was a short, wiry man with a mustache and goatee. If he had been wearing a silk weskit and smoking jacket, he would have been *Masterpiece Theatre* for sure. But he had on a worn pair of corduroy pants and a rumpled button-down shirt, open at the collar and topped with a V-necked sweater. There were old canvas deck shoes on his feet.

He shuffled on out to his kitchen and turned on the light as we tagged along behind.

"Kicked you out, did they?" he asked.

I stared at him, then at Pamela and Elizabeth. "We didn't even knock," I said.

"Eh?" he said, one hand to his ear. I noticed the hearing aid and repeated my answer.

The kitchen was almost as large as the living room, with cupboards all the way to the ceiling. Mr. Watts began handing plates and glasses to Pamela, and she dutifully set them on the table.

Somehow I'd thought that maybe Mr. Watts would phone upstairs and tell Lester we were there, tell him about the dinner we had brought, and that Lester would come get us. Then it wouldn't look so much as though we'd crashed his party. But now it was clear that Mr. Watts was going to do no such thing. Elizabeth and Pamela watched in astonishment.

"Well, I figured as much," the old man went on, rummaging now through the silverware drawer and handing a serving spoon to Elizabeth. "Didn't know you were coming, did they?"

"How did you know that?" I asked, speaking more loudly.

He smiled, and his watery blue eyes sparkled. "The first contingent brought wine and cheesecake at six thirty, and I could smell Lester's shrimp in oyster sauce around seven. I figured they had about all they needed to eat right there. Then you girls showed up, and it was just the way you got out of the car and crept up those steps that told me you weren't exactly on the guest list. Which one of you is Alice?"

He even knew my name!

"She is," said Elizabeth, pointing.

Mr. Watts's eyes twinkled again. "I won't tell Lester you were here if you won't tell him I ate lasagna," he said. "Cholesterol, you know." And we all sat down at the table. We figured it was better than sitting on the steps in the cold, waiting for Pamela's mother to come back and pick us up.

"So what are you? Some kind of spy—watching out the window all the time?" Pamela kidded.

"CIA," the old man said, just above a whisper, and lifted a forkful of salad to his lips. The back of his hand was covered with brown age spots. "Yep. Knew Berlin backward and forward. All hush-hush business, of course. Not even supposed to talk about it now." He picked up the serving spoon. "Lasagna, anyone?"

As he put some on each plate Pamela said, "I'll bet you were a dashing spy in a long trench coat, with a woman on each arm."

Mr. Watts laughed. "All but the trench coat," he said, the last word ending in a wheeze. And then, while we ate our dinner and sliced the cake (Mr. Watts ate two pieces), he told us how he had almost been trapped by a female named Matilda, who, of course, was spying on him in turn, and how he'd escaped only by crawling through the skylight of a building, which he was able to do because he'd been on the gymnastics team at Georgetown University.

We almost hated to leave when the meal was over, but I noticed after a while that Mr. Watts was nodding off with a cup of coffee still in his hand. It was probably already past his bedtime.

So Pamela called her mom, and after we had used Mr. Watts's bathroom and come out again, I saw that he had successfully removed all the left-over lasagna from our dish, emptied the rest of the salad into a container of his own, and transferred the remains of the cake to a pie tin and was putting it all in his fridge.

"Got my dinner for the next three nights," he said. "Awful nice of you girls to come by." And when Mrs. Jones drove up, he walked us to the door and said, "Next time call your brother first." He winked. "He may have a Matilda up there him-self, who knows?"

We were still laughing about it when we reached the car and told Mrs. Jones the whole story. She thought it was funny too.

"You should have called me sooner!" she kept saying. "I could have come over and had dinner with you."

Maybe we should have, but we'd wanted it to be our own adventure. It's hard when a parent is lonely and wants to be all buddy-buddy with you.

No matter how hard they try, they can never be one of the gang, no matter how hip they are, and you don't really want them to.

"Do you girls want to come over and see how I've decorated my apartment?" she asked. "It's sort of fifties-style art deco. I've even got one of those metal turquoise dinette sets."

"Oh, not tonight, Mom. We're staying over at Elizabeth's," Pamela said.

Mrs. Jones didn't answer for a moment. Then she said, "Well, sometime, then. And I'll do all the cooking. Anything you want."

"Thanks, Mom," said Pamela.

"Darn!" Elizabeth sprawled on her bed in her flannel drawstring PJs with the tiny blue flowers on them. "I thought we were going to have a fun evening with Lester."

"Me too," I said. I sat across from her on the other bed, making a braid in my hair. "Gwen was right when she said we can't just walk in on a bunch of guys. Who knows what they might have been doing."

"I wonder if that will ever be us, all living in the same apartment together, having people in," mused Pamela.

"Let's all go to the same college!" Elizabeth said enthusiastically.

"I may go to a theater arts school or something," Pamela told her.

"Couldn't we be together for just one year, all in the same room at a college?" Elizabeth pleaded.

"I don't think you can choose your own roommates at college," I told her. "They like to mix people up."

We looked at each other in dismay.

"Then let's promise that none of us will get married and move away till we've become career women and lived together, *some*place, for one year," said Elizabeth.

I thought that over. "How can we promise anything?" I said slowly. "Remember how we used to think we'd get married at the same time, have our babies at the same time? You can't control stuff like that."

We lay on our stomachs on the twin beds, chins resting on our arms. Pamela began to smile.

"I know one thing we could all do at the same time," she said.

"Do I want to hear this, Pamela?" I asked.

"*What?*" asked Elizabeth.

"Lose our virginity," said Pamela.

"Pamela!" Elizabeth said.

"You know. Prom night. Isn't that when a lot of girls do it? If we're with guys we like, I mean," said Pamela.

I looked at her. "Just because it's prom night? In the backseat of a car?"

"No. We could all rent a hotel room. That's what some kids do."

"Sure isn't the way I imagined it," I said.

"What? You wanted music? We could have music. You wanted wine? We could get some wine."

Elizabeth looked thoughtful. "Would you turn out the lights?" she asked.

Now I stared at Elizabeth. "You're *considering* this?"

"I just want to know the particulars," said Elizabeth. "Do you take turns in the bed or what?"

I rolled over on my back. "I'm not even part of this conversation," I said.

"One couple at a time, Liz, of course!" Pamela said. "The rest of us could stand out in the hall or go in the bathroom or something."

"The *bathroom*?" Elizabeth said.

"Is there one sane person in this room?" I asked. "You want to go back to school the following Monday and hear the guys talk about who scored? You want to be a *score*?"

"I'd like *some*thing exciting to happen in my life, other than listening to my parents fight," said Pamela.

I'd already been thinking about this—about

how to get Pamela involved in something fun. "You know what I'm going to do? I'm going to sign you up for the Drama Club next semester," I announced. She'd quit after only a few months last year, but I don't give up so easily.

"I don't think I'm good enough," she protested. "My voice, I mean. In case there's a singing part."

"Don't give me that!" I said. "You're taking voice lessons. It won't hurt you to try out." I looked to Elizabeth for support.

Liz nodded. "You're as good as some of the girls who were in *Fiddler* last spring. Alice is right, Pamela. You'd be great."

Pamela shrugged, then grinned. "I'd be great on prom night, too."

But I noticed she hadn't said no. And I made up my mind that if she didn't put her name on the sign-up sheet in January, I'd do it for her. But Pamela pushes the envelope sometimes, and she just wouldn't quit talking about having sex on prom night.

"Whether you think you would or not, Liz, you'd better go to the prom prepared, because it's usually on the guy's mind," she said.

"So I'll go to the prom prepared *not* to have sex, Pamela. I'm not going to do it just because a guy wants it. That's the way girls get into trouble," Elizabeth said.

"Liz, you can go to a party with no intention of getting involved with someone," said Pamela, "and the next thing you know, some guy has his hand down your pants and—"

"I've already thought of that."

"And?" I said, curious.

"You've got to have a backup," she told us. "The point is never to go anyplace without a friend. Let's say you're my backup, Alice, and we go to a party where a guy comes over and tries to push me into a bedroom. We'd have this signal, see. Like, if I blink twice, it means, 'Things are heating up; keep an eye on us.' If I crook my little finger, it means, 'Come over and interrupt.' And—"

The cordless phone between the beds rang, and Liz picked it up. All at once we saw her face soften, her lips curve into a pleased smile. Then we heard her say, "Hi, Ross."

Pamela and I bolted straight up.

Elizabeth smiled and cupped one hand over the phone, turning away from us. "Yes," she said softly. "Me too . . . every night. *Especially* before I go to sleep."

Pamela and I began gesturing wildly. Elizabeth turned around and looked at us. We began blinking our eyes and crooking our little fingers and panting and—

Elizabeth laughed. And then, into the phone,

she said, "There are two insane girls here, that's all. . . . Right! Alice and Pamela. How did you guess?"

At the Melody Inn the next day I was rearranging the silk scarves in the display case of the Gift Shoppe under the stairs—the scarves with composers' signatures making a design on the fabric—but I was watching David, the new employee, helping a customer choose a songbook.

"Does David have a girlfriend?" I asked Marilyn.

"How could he not?" she answered with a wink. "Every female customer who comes in here dawdles when she sees David. Why? You interested?"

"Too busy," I said. "I haven't got time for a boyfriend."

"That I don't believe for one minute," said Marilyn.

I just wasn't sure I wanted to get involved with someone who worked for Dad, though. It would be awkward being in the same store, especially if we quarreled or anything. But I'll bet Pamela would be interested.

During a lull in business that afternoon, David and I were talking near the back of the store by the watercooler.

"So what do you do for fun, David?" I asked

"Well, I sing in a men's chorus; I ski; fool around on my computer. . . . I'm trying to make some life choices, that's all."

"Now, that sounds serious."

"Well, it can be."

"No girlfriend?" I asked, smiling.

"Not at the moment," he said, and smiled back.

When I e-mailed Pamela about David later and told her how good-looking he is, she was online and sent me an instant message in reply:

I'll bet he's gay.

Me: Why would you think that?

Pamela: Because when the boss's daughter comes on to him the way you did and he doesn't bite, there's got to be a reason.

Me: Well, it could be that he doesn't have a lot of money, or I don't turn him on, or . . .

Pamela: We've got to find out.

Me: If I turn him on?

Pamela: If *girls* turn him on. PROJECT DAVID! Let's take him out, the three of us.

I forwarded our conversation to Elizabeth.

Elizabeth: Yeah?

she typed back.

Look what happened with PROJECT LESTER.
I'll do it, though.

Me: You guys are nuts,

I told them. But I knew David was in for it now.

I had other things to think about, though. I still had that ugly, stupid, exasperating embroidery to finish, and it was eating at me. I wished I'd never started it. I knew that Sylvia was busy in the kitchen, however, and would be there for a while, so I got out the thread once again to see if I couldn't finish another flower. But this time I did a petal and a half before I realized I had stitched both sides of the pillowcase together and would have to take out all I had just done.

"Dammit!" I cried angrily, and threw the pillow-case across the room as tears rose up in my eyes. Then I sat breathing hard, trying to calm myself until I got up the courage to try again. I went over and picked up the pillowcase, then pricked my finger on the needle, getting a small bloodstain on the fabric.

"Stupid! Stupid! Stupid!" I wept, thinking what

a dumb idea this had been. Why couldn't I have bought them a silver serving spoon or a teapot or something? Why did I feel I had to make something when I've never been very good at handicrafts?

By Sunday night, though, I'd finished. It was an amateurish job, but it certainly showed effort and persistence. I'd managed to wash out the blood-stain, and I pressed the sheet and washed the one pillowcase that seemed most dirty. Then I folded them carefully, wrapped them in tissue paper, and put them in a brown box with an ivory ribbon around it. Dad and Sylvia had gone to bed early, and I decided to give it to them the next night at dinner.

When the phone rang, I picked it up immediately so as not to wake them. It was Lester.

"So when did you start bringing pineapple upside-down cake to Mr. Watts?" he asked.

"What?" I said. "How did you know? He said he wouldn't tell!"

"Aha! He didn't. I went down yesterday to check on him and found him eating a piece of pineapple upside-down cake with all the pecans turned on their sides in a circle pattern. Nobody makes pineapple upside-down cake like that except you." He paused. "Why did you bring it over? All I could get out of him was, 'My lips are sealed.'"

"It was just a present," I said, deciding he didn't have to know more.

"He was eating lasagna, too, Al."

"So?"

"He never makes lasagna."

"Maybe he bought it."

"And a salad with artichokes in it. He picked up an artichoke and asked me what it was. Somebody brought him a whole dinner, Al—all the stuff he's not supposed to eat."

I lost it then. "It was supposed to be a surprise, Lester! But when we got to your door, we—"

"*My* door? Who's 'we'?"

"Pamela and Elizabeth and me."

"When?"

"Friday night. And Elizabeth thought you were having an orgy."

"*What?*"

"Because of the woman in her slip."

"That was a dress, Al."

"Yeah, I know. I'm just yanking your chain."

"How did you get over here?"

"Pamela's mother dropped us off."

"What were you trying to do?"

"Surprise you! Bring you your dinner. We didn't know you were having a party."

"Hey, Al. Call first, will you?"

"I know, I know. I don't need a sermon from you too."

I told him the whole story. Lester was quiet a

moment, then he said, "Well, it was a nice thought, anyway, and I'm sorry the evening was such a bust for you."

I didn't want him feeling sorry for us or I'd feel even more stupid and childish than I did. "It wasn't a bust, it was fun. We had a lovely dinner, and Mr. Watts told us all about his life as a spy."

"A spy?"

"S-P-Y. He's been to Berlin, even!"

"Berlin, Maryland," said Lester. "As far as I know, he's never been out of the United States."

"But he's worked for the CIA!"

"Right! Center for Insecticide Advancement or something like that. Man oh man, did he ever do a number on you!"

"But . . . but . . . he said it all had to be secret."

"He studied infestations, Alice. And naturally, no one especially cares to have that broadcast around."

"And he almost got trapped by Matilda and escaped through a skylight and—"

Lester laughed long and hard. "Matilda was somebody's dog!"

"What?" I said. "Then why did he *tell* us all that stuff?"

"Probably his way of thanking you for the dinner. He entertained you, didn't he?" said Lester.

• • •

I told Pamela and Elizabeth and Gwen about it the next day, and we had a good laugh.

"If he wasn't a spy, he should have been," said Pamela. "He could make anyone believe anything."

When I got off the bus with Elizabeth that afternoon, we started down the street to her house. I was going to stay over there for a while so we could study for the algebra test when Elizabeth slowed suddenly and asked, "Isn't that a moving van in front of your house?"

I stared hard as we got a little closer. There was a huge white truck parked out front, and two men were coming down the steps, each carrying a large carton.

"If I didn't know better, I'd say it looks like someone's moving out," said Elizabeth.

"But there's no one there!" I said, walking a little faster. "Dad's at work and Sylvia's at school and—"

But the front door was wide open, and standing just inside was . . . Sylvia.

14

More Changes

"Sylvia's leaving?" I said, aghast. Would she just come home in the middle of the afternoon and clear out before Dad got here? How could this be?

"Did they have a fight?" asked Elizabeth.

We stood transfixed on the sidewalk in front of Elizabeth's house, and then we saw the two men emerge from the back of the van carrying something *in,* Sylvia holding the door open for them.

"We're idiots," said Elizabeth. "It's a *delivery* truck."

I began to wonder if I was spending too much time with Elizabeth Price. Lately, I'd even begun to sound like her. Maybe that's what happens when you hang around too long with the same people; you sound like your best friends.

"I think I'll study at home," I said. "If Sylvia's moving stuff around, I'd like to be there."

"E-mail me later," Liz said, and went on up the

steps, where her little brother was waving at her from the window.

I crossed the street and went inside. The men were hoisting a huge rectangular package up the stairs, the man below supporting it on his shoulder.

"Oh, Alice!" Sylvia said when she saw me. "I came home early because they're delivering the Christmas present Ben and I are giving each other."

"Already?" I said, curious.

"Yes. We bought a new bedroom set, and it's gorgeous. We didn't want to wait till Christmas to enjoy it. You could help me get it all ready before your dad gets home, if you like."

"Okay!" I said. "Wow! All these changes!"

"Sort of makes your head swim, doesn't it?" she said.

We got out of the way when the men came down again, carrying the empty wrapper, and finally, after Sylvia signed the delivery papers, we scurried upstairs for a look.

What a difference it made in Dad's room! Instead of his old bed and chest of drawers, there was a brand-new mattress set and headboard, two nightstands, a new chest of drawers, and a long dresser with six drawers and a tall mirror attached at one end. I noticed Dad's old desk had stayed in the room, and then I saw a smaller, narrow chest with eight shallow drawers in it. I'd never seen something like that.

"What's the little chest for?" I asked, pulling out the top drawer.

Sylvia grinned. "Lingerie," she said. "Slips in one, bras in another, panty hose, nighties. . . . We really should say that this is not only our Christmas present to each other, but Valentine's Day and birthdays, too!"

"It's beautiful!" I said, running my hand along the top of the long dresser, the wood's grain the color of wheat. "What did you do with Dad's old stuff?"

"It's in Lester's room, and that will be the guest room. Right now it's squeezed in there along with his twin bed, but we'll think of something."

I stood looking around. "The room sure seems smaller with all this in it," I said.

"I know. But when we build the addition, we can move Ben's desk down to the new study. I think it will work."

The phone rang just then, and Sylvia went out in the hall to answer. I wandered over to the bed and sat down on the soft new pillow-top mattress. I could hear Sylvia talking to Dad. "Yes, darling, it came, and you're going to love it," she was saying.

But suddenly my eyes fell on the mattress label: BEAUTY REST, it read. QUEEN SIZE.

I felt a dull hollowness in my chest, my throat growing tighter. I got up and walked down the hall, past Sylvia, into my own room, and shut the door behind me. The set of bed linens I had bought and spent weeks and weeks embroidering was for a double-size bed, Dad's old bed. I curled up against my pillow, angry tears in my eyes. All that time I had been working on that set, all the stitches I had taken out and restitched! The evenings I had stayed up far past my usual bed-time to get it done, and they had gone out and bought a different size bed!

Sylvia tapped on my door. "Alice? Ready to help me make the bed? I bought new sheets, a new bedspread, and matching drapes."

I struggled to sound normal. "I guess I can't," I called out. "I really should study for a test."

There was silence outside the bedroom. "Sure?" she asked finally.

"Yeah," I said.

More silence. She tapped lightly again. "Alice? Is anything wrong?"

"Of course not," I lied.

At last she said, "All right. I'll surprise you too, then, and you can see it all done when your dad gets home."

I hated myself then, but it didn't stop the anger. And I was also angry at the way I sulk sometimes and don't say what's wrong. "You're not made of glass," Dad told me once. "I don't know what's the matter unless you tell me." But how could I tell a new stepmom that she'd just ruined the gift I'd worked on for so long? How could I say that things were happening too fast and that ever since she came, nothing had been the same? It was as though I was in a snit and couldn't shake it—as though I'd fallen into a well, and no matter how hard I tried, I couldn't climb out.

I guess I couldn't believe they would have gone out and bought a whole bedroom set without even mentioning it to me. Always before, Dad and Lester told me everything that was about to happen to our house. I even knew when we were going to paint a room or buy a new toilet seat!

When Dad came home, I heard his footsteps on the stairs. Heard him exclaim over the new spread and drapes. Heard him sliding drawers open and closed.

"Looks even better here than it did in the showroom," he said.

"Isn't the spread perfect, Ben?" Sylvia said. "See how the wood picks up the background color in the drapes?"

"Alice!" Dad called. "Sylvia and I are celebrating Christmas early. Come and see what we got."

I tried hard to fake enthusiasm as I went down

the hall to their room. "I already saw the furniture," I said, opening and closing a drawer. "The
spread's nice." And then, because I was afraid I
might bawl, I left the room, went to my own, and
took their wedding present from my closet, all
wrapped and tied with ivory ribbon. I went back
to their bedroom, where they were still staring
after me, and tossed it onto their bed.

"Your wedding present," I said. "I finally got it
done." Then I went down the hall and closed my
door.

There was only silence from their room. Finally
I heard the sound of tissue paper rustling.
Murmurs. And all the while I sat on the edge of
my bed staring out the window, angry, embarrassed tears rolling down my stupid cheeks.

I didn't know who I was angriest at—Dad and
Sylvia or myself for being such a dork. I heard my
door opening behind me, and they both came in,
but I wouldn't turn around.

"This is something you've been working on for
a long time, right?" Dad said. "It's really a gift from
the heart, Al. Thank you."

I just sniffled.

"The colors are gorgeous, Alice," said Sylvia. "I
love them! I've never had monogrammed sheets
before. It was really thoughtful of you!"

I still wouldn't look at them, but I heard myself

say, "Well, it might have been thoughtful if you guys had told me you were buying a queen-size bed, because after all my work, they won't fit."

"Only the bottom sheet," said Sylvia, coming around where she could see my face, but I turned away. "We can easily buy another one of those to match."

"The top sheet won't look right," I said angrily. "It will barely cover you."

Dad walked around my bed too and sat down a few feet away. I felt like a specimen in a petri dish, the way they were both studying me, and knew my nose was red from crying. My nose is always the giveaway.

"Well, we'll make it work!" he said brightly. "We could save this set for our guest room. They'll fit perfectly on my old bed."

"I didn't *make* them for a guest room, I made them for *you*!" I said. "If you'd just let me in on what's going on around here once in a while, I might have bought the right size to begin with."

I couldn't believe I was talking like that in front of Sylvia! Couldn't believe my voice could sound so shaky.

"We have several options," Sylvia said finally. "You didn't embroider the fitted sheet, so that's no problem to replace. I can use just the top sheet and the pillowcases for our new bed, or we could put both sheets in the guest room but save the pillowcases for us alone. Then we can enjoy your embroidery, and so can our guests."

That did seem the best solution, but it didn't solve everything.

"It doesn't solve the way you two just go ahead and do things without telling me," I said.

"Al," said Dad, and I thought I sensed impatience in his voice. Embarrassment even, at the way I was acting. "If we had known what you were planning, we certainly would have told you *our* plans. But I really don't think that the size bed we wanted to buy was something we felt we had to share with you."

I could feel my cheeks burning. It really ticked me off. "It's not just that! You made plans to remodel the house and didn't tell me about that, either. You turned Lester's room into a guest room before I knew anything about it. You went off on your honeymoon without even saying good-bye. Suddenly I'm just the third wheel around here."

If I thought they were going to sit down on either side of me and hug me and tell me how important I was to the family, I was mistaken. Sylvia leaned against my dresser, still holding the pillowcases in her hand, and Dad just stared out the window with me.

"I guess the changes aren't all to the house," he

said. "There are also going to be changes in the way we do things, and maybe this is a good time to talk about it. Because this was a present between Sylvia and me, we didn't feel we needed to run it by you first."

He waited, and when I still didn't say anything, he said, "I know how disappointed you must be after all the work you put into your present, Al. But we'll make good use of the set, and we really do appreciate it."

I began to feel like a third grader then, a pouting sulky kid of eight.

"Okay," I said in a small voice. "I didn't mean to act so juvenile."

"Well, I still say they're beautiful," said Sylvia. "And I'm going to sleep very well tonight with my head on an embroidered pillowcase."

We talked a little while longer, and then they went downstairs. But it was all so academic sounding. All so buddy-buddy, so understanding. Maybe I would have felt better if I had yelled at them and they had yelled back and we got some *real* feelings going here. Even when we were mad at each other, we were still too polite. We just didn't sound like *family*.

I made a mistake telling my girlfriends about David, the hot new employee at the Melody Inn.

Because Karen said she stopped by one day after school and got a good look at him, then Pamela did, and when I went to work the following Saturday, Marilyn told me that there had been a parade of girls coming by all week.

"That first one couldn't have been more obvious," she said.

"Who was she?" I asked.

"I don't know. Tall, light brown hair, *very* sexy, and probably a 34C. Maybe even a D."

"Jill," I said. "It had to be Jill."

"Well, I wish you'd tell them to lay off. I think they're making David uncomfortable," Marilyn said.

"I didn't tell anyone to come in!" I said. "I *did* tell them he was hot, though. I guess I shouldn't have."

"Duh!" said Marilyn.

"So . . . did he flirt with any of them?"

"David is very professional, and that's one of the reasons we hired him," Marilyn said. "I think your busty friend was disappointed that he didn't fall all over her."

"That's Jill, all right," I said, and laughed.

Around three fifteen, just after Marilyn had gone on her break, Dad was on the second floor filling in for a violin instructor who was sick and David and I were trying to run the store ourselves when

I saw a whole scouting party, you might say, approaching the store for the second time. There they were: Jill, Karen, Pamela, and—believe it or not—Amy Sheldon. I had a sinking feeling in my stomach. I could tell by the look on Jill's face that she was up to no good.

They stood just inside the door, pretending to look at a rack of CDs while David waited on a customer, but Amy was the focus of their attention. I would have gone over, but I had a customer who had asked to try on a pair of tiny piano-shaped earrings from the gift wheel, and with something as small as an earring, you don't walk off and leave a customer alone.

The woman at David's counter paid for her selection and left the store, and I saw Karen nudge Amy forward. I tried to catch Pamela's eye, but she wouldn't look at me—on purpose, I'm sure.

Amy went across the store while the other girls watched.

"Pamela!" I hissed, but she pretended not to hear.

After my customer had paid for the earrings, the other girls came over to the Gift Shoppe, crowding around the counter and watching Amy.

"What are you guys up to?" I asked.

"This is going to be a riot!" said Jill. "I told Amy that there's this guy at the Melody Inn who watches her pass the store each day on her way home—she lives in those apartments on the next block—and that he's been dying to meet her. I said she ought to come in and introduce herself, and she *is*! She'll fall for anything."

"You told her that David's interested in her? Jill, how could you? That was cruel!" I said, remembering all too well the remark *I'd* made about Amy.

"Oh, she's so thick, she won't even get it," said Karen. "But at least we'll find out his love-life status. *I* told her I think he's gay."

"Karen, that's none of our business!" I said.

"It is if we want to go out with him," she told me. "Jill practically fell in his lap, and he didn't bite. He's *got* to be gay."

"Did it ever occur to you that maybe some guys . . . ?" I didn't finish, because our eyes were glued on Amy. She was leaning her elbows on the counter in the sheet music department. The fuchsia sweater I'd seen her wear at school on special occasions wasn't a color that looked particularly good on her, but she had obviously curled her hair that morning and had it delicately framing her face.

"Look at her!" Karen said, laughing. "Giving him the ol' bug eyes!"

"And look at the way he's backing up!" added Pamela, giggling. "I'll bet he wishes there were a trapdoor under her and a button he could press."

But David didn't seem to be trying to get away. In fact, he was backing up to sit on a high stool that Marilyn kept behind the counter, as though he'd like to continue their conversation. There were all sorts of excuses he could have made if he'd wanted to get away from Amy, all sorts of places he could hide. But he didn't. And then we saw him study Amy for a minute and smile.

We were flabbergasted.

"If she gets a date with him, I'm going to be sick," said Jill.

I remembered what Karen had told me last summer about Jill and Justin having sex. "I thought you and Justin were . . . uh . . . involved," I said.

"So?" Jill said, and laughed. She pretended to be looking at jewelry on the gift wheel, but I knew she was straining to hear the conversation between Amy and David. Every time David looked our way, the girls started talking with each other.

Marilyn came out of the stockroom then, where she'd taken her coffee. She looked at me and then at my friends. "You want to take your break, Alice?" she said. "Why don't you go now, and then I'll let David go."

I was glad to get out of there and take the girls with me. Dad and Marilyn don't like my friends hanging around the store when I'm working on

Saturdays. We lingered just long enough to signal to Amy that we would be in the coffee shop next door. We saw her straighten up and smile at David. Then we saw her lean over the counter and kiss him on the cheek.

"Oh . . . my . . . God!" said Jill.

Amy came toward us, smiling, and we practically dragged her out the door and into the coffee shop. We gathered around a table in one corner.

"What *happened*?" Karen said. "Did he ask you out?"

"No. I asked *him* out," said Amy.

"*What?*" we all cried together.

"If he said yes, I *know* I'm going to be sick," said Jill.

Amy sat back and touched one hand to her lips, as though remembering the kiss. "He said no," she told us.

"Where were you going to take him?" I asked, curious, feeling a secret admiration for Amy Sheldon.

"I asked him if he liked to Rollerblade, and he said yes, so I told him I knew a rink where we could go, and he said that it sounded like fun but that he was afraid he couldn't."

"Did he say why?" asked Pamela. We all waited to hear.

"Well, I asked him if he was gay, and—"

"Amy, you didn't!" I said.

"You actually asked him that?" Jill said.

"Yes, and he said no," Amy went on. "He said he broke up with a longtime girlfriend recently because he's thinking about becoming a priest, and he doesn't want to get involved with anyone else right now."

We sat in silent awe of Amy Sheldon. She couldn't have been with David the Hottie for more than five or six minutes, but she found out more about him than the rest of us could in a week. Just by being Amy.

"A priest!" Karen said finally, disappointed. "What a waste!"

I thought of how David must have sensed what was going on, must have realized that Amy was sort of the ugly duckling and that the other girls had put her up to talking to him. Of how kind he'd been to her. "Oh, I don't know," I said. "I think maybe he'd make a very good priest."

"A guy that good-looking shouldn't be allowed to be a priest!" said Jill. "I think one of us ought to come in every week for the next six months and ask him out so he won't make the mistake of a life-time."

But it was Amy who had the last word: "How do you know it wouldn't be the mistake of a lifetime to take *you* out?" she said simply.

We gasped, and Pamela gave a little whistle.

"Well, maybe I had that coming," Jill said, and laughed uncomfortably.

"Just because he wouldn't talk to you, Jill, doesn't mean that guys won't talk to me," Amy added, a little defiantly.

And then I saw a way to redeem myself with Amy Sheldon. "He never says much to me, either, Amy, and I see him every Saturday," I said. "Maybe there's something about you that makes guys want to open up and confide."

Amy looked at me, and a slow smile spread across her face. "I guess so," she said, "because he's taking his coffee break in fifteen minutes, and he said he'd buy me a Coke."

Karen and Jill and Pamela sat dumbfounded, but I raised one fist in the air. "Go, Amy!" I said, and then we all laughed.

Somehow she would do all right, I thought.

I was checking my e-mail that evening when an IM popped up from somebody using the screen name ZooGirl.

Who? I thought, and clicked READ. Rosalind! Who else?

Rosalind: Hey! That you, Alice?

Me: Rosalind! I should have known! It was

so great to see you at Dad's store in October! How'd you get my e-mail address?

Rosalind: Oh, I just messed around till I found it. We've got a lot of catching up to do.

Me: I know. I've got a million things to ask you. Major, major questions, like what happened to Jody and Dawn and Megan, and are you going out with anyone?

Rosalind: Guess.

Me: Guess who you're going out with?

Rosalind: Yeah.

Me: Somebody I know?

Rosalind: Could be.

Me: Donald Sheavers?

Rosalind: Are you crazy?

Me: Is it a guy? Not an elephant . . . !

Rosalind: LOL. It's a guy.

Me: I give up.

Rosalind: Remember Ollie?

Me: Ollie???!!! The boy who was always trying to kiss us?

Rosalind: Kiss you, you mean! He remembers.

Me: Wow! What's he like?

Rosalind: You want me to describe his kisses?

Me: Listen, we've got to get together.

Rosalind: Yeah. I've got a test to study for this week. After the first of the year, maybe? I'll drop by the Melody Inn some Saturday, and we'll have lunch. Mark your calendar.

After we had signed off, I sat smiling to myself. Ollie and Rosalind! Who would have thought? And he still remembered me. I wondered what he'd think of me now if he saw me with braces.

15

Truly Disgusting

A week before Christmas, two days before winter break, I woke up feeling dizzy. I thought maybe I'd just got up from bed too fast when my alarm went off, but by the time I got to the bathroom, I felt even worse. I had that queasy feeling you get when you might throw up, and it felt as though my intestines were rolling around inside me.

When you first realize you're sick, you think of all the reasons you shouldn't be. You *can't* be. I had to turn in an English assignment; I wanted to wear my suede boots; Gwen was going to show me the bracelet she'd got from Joe Ortega—the guy she'd met at camp. . . .

I leaned over the toilet, but nothing happened. That's an even worse feeling than going ahead and puking.

I made my way to the top of the stairs. "Dad?" I called feebly.

A chair scraped in the kitchen, and Dad came to the foot of the staircase. "Yes?"

"I don't feel so good. I think I'd better stay home," I told him.

"Really, Al?" He took a few steps more so he could see me better. "What's wrong?"

"Stomach flu or something."

"Oh, I'm sorry. Did you take your temperature?" he asked.

I braced one hand against the wall, feeling dizzy again. "No, but I will. Could you ask Elizabeth to turn in my English assignment for me? It's inside my three-ring binder on the coffee table."

"All right," Dad said. "Maybe I should stay home with you."

"I'll be okay," I said, not feeling okay at all.

Dad seemed unsure. "Sylvia had to go in early this morning for a meeting, and I've got a new instructor to interview, but I could cancel. . . ."

"If I need you, I'll call you at work, but I can get along by myself," I said. "I just want to go back to bed."

"Take your temperature first. If it's as high as one hundred and one, I'm calling Dr. Beverly," Dad said.

I found the thermometer and crawled back under the covers with it in my mouth. It was still there when Dad came into the room a few minutes later. "It's just over one hundred," he said, checking. "Can I bring you anything before I leave? Orange juice?"

I put one hand over my mouth. "Don't even mention food. I just want to sleep."

"I don't know, Al. . . ."

"Karen and Brian and a lot of other kids at school had the flu last week. I'm sure that's what this is," I said.

"All right. I'll drop by at noon and look in on you," said Dad.

I pulled the blanket up under my chin. My mouth felt like it was full of cotton balls. "Don't forget to give Liz my assignment," I murmured.

"I'll take it over right now," Dad told me.

I woke up once to get a bucket from under the sink and put it beside the bed, just in case, but I didn't throw up. I had the runs instead. I sat on the toilet and decided I would probably be there all day.

When I got off at last, I drank some water and went back to bed, but I'd only been there five minutes before I had to go again. I didn't make it. I sat on the toilet, the room spinning around, and this time when I flushed, I left my soiled pajama bottoms in a heap in one corner and wobbled back to bed, so dizzy I was afraid I might fall over. I thought about calling Dad, but I felt if I could just get under the covers, I could sleep away the afternoon.

The pillow felt cool against my cheek, and I was pretty sure my temperature had gone up some more. I felt myself drifting off into an uneasy dream, as though I was going in and out of sleep.

I'm not sure how long I lay there, but I could hear footsteps moving softly around in the hallway. I figured it must be noon at least, maybe one o'clock. It was comforting to know that Dad was there watching over me. Once I felt, or dreamed that I felt, his hand on my forehead, but I didn't even open my eyes. Finally, when I woke completely, it was two forty-five, and I could hear rustling from downstairs. I figured that Dad had taken the rest of the day off.

There was a tall glass of water on my nightstand, and I drank half of it, but that was a mistake, I guess. I got up and hurried to the bathroom, realizing I was now wearing the tops of my pajamas and nothing on below. I sat on the toilet seat again, holding my head in my hands, and finally, when I flushed, I saw that my dirty pajama bottoms were gone.

Yuck! I thought. Dad had got the job of dealing with them. I rinsed out my mouth, wrapped a bath towel around me in case I met Dad in the hall, and opened the bathroom door. I came face-to-face with Sylvia, coming up the stairs.

"Oh!" I said, embarrassed.

"Ben called me at school to tell me you were sick, and I told him we had assembly this afternoon, so I could take care of you. Mr. Ormand's got my sixth-period class. How are you, sweetheart?"

How was I? I didn't feel like anyone's sweetheart, that's for sure. I stood there holding a towel around me, wondering whether I looked even worse than I smelled.

"Awful," I mumbled. "I've been running to the bathroom all day." And then I realized it was *Sylvia* who had found my soiled pajama bottoms! I couldn't stand it. I stumbled on into my room and crawled under the covers, still holding the towel around me.

She came in, wearing jeans and a sweater and loafers, and sat on the edge of my bed. Placing one hand on my forehead, she said, "I called the doctor, and he told me you have the same classic symptoms he's been seeing all week. I know that doesn't make you feel any better, but he said the worst is usually over in twenty-four hours."

"I'm a mess," I said.

"You're supposed to be! That's what sick's all about," she said.

What a weird way to put it. Like I was doing what I was supposed to do! Look and smell disgusting!

"When you think you might like a little ginger ale, I'll bring some up," she said. "I'm going to fix you an ice bag, too. That might feel good against your cheek. Sleep now, if you can."

I was glad she left so I could get up and put on some underpants. Then I slept for several hours, and when I woke, there was an ice bag next to my face, a glass of ginger ale on the nightstand, and down at the foot of my bed, my pajama bottoms, all clean and folded, still slightly warm from the dryer.

The first call I got, strangely, was from Penny. When Dad came home, he placed the hall phone beside my bed so I wouldn't have to get up to talk. Other families, see, have cordless phones and cell phones, but we're still back in the Dark Ages. A phone upstairs, a phone down, and Dad thinks we're big time.

"Hi," Penny said. "I'll bet you feel as awful as I did last week."

"I didn't know you'd been sick too."

"It was over the weekend, so I didn't miss any school. How you doing?" she asked.

"Pretty yucky. Sick at both ends," I told her.

"Isn't that the worst? Everyone was asking about you today, and Liz said she turned in your English assignment. If we get any assignments tomorrow, we'll get them to you, but seeing that it's the last day before vacation, I don't think that'll happen."

"Hope not," I said.

"Well, you'll be okay in a day or two. I was, anyway. Have a great Christmas!" she told me.

"Thanks. Hope you have a good one too," I said. Was it possible that we weren't pretending anymore? I wondered. That, if we weren't *close* friends, we were at least friends?

I had just put the phone down when Liz called. "How're you feeling?" she asked.

"Putrid," I said. "Somebody ought to put a 'Caution: Blasting Zone' sign near my rear end."

She laughed. "Patrick asked about you."

"Good for Patrick," I said.

"Everyone's afraid to call in case you're sleeping."

"Everyone's afraid I'll be on the john, that's why," I corrected her. "Oops! Got to go again."

"Bye," she said quickly, and hung up.

Dad brought up the *Post* comics when I returned to bed. "Sylvia has to be at school tomorrow, but I can be here all day," he said.

"You won't have to, because I know I'll be better," I told him.

I slept through the dinner hour, and when I

woke, my pillow was damp with perspiration, but I did feel better. I went to the bathroom again, then came back and sat on the edge of my bed, drinking the ginger ale and contemplating my clean pajama bottoms, wondering if I dared put them on. When I put the glass back down, I saw Lester standing in the doorway looking at me.

"Lester!" I scolded, scooting back under the blanket.

"I couldn't tell if it was a girl in her underpants or one of the witches out of *Macbeth*," he said. "Do you feel as bad as you look?"

"You're not helping," I said. "Go away."

"Just came by to see what you wanted for Christmas, actually," he said. "Bedpan? Pajamas, maybe? A jug of Listerine?"

"Just go away!" I repeated. "Besides, I'm probably contagious."

"Why do you think I'm standing twenty feet off?" he said. "But seriously, what *do* you want for Christmas? Within reason, of course."

"What I would *really* like won't cost you a cent," I told him.

"That's my kind of present!" said Lester.

"You won't even have to wrap it," I said.

"Sounds better all the time."

"Well, now that you mention it, it's a gift of time."

Lester stopped smiling. "Do *not* ask me to take Pamela out because she's feeling depressed lately."

"No. I want you to teach me to drive."

"Arrrrrrrggggggghhhhhh!" said Lester, clutching his head.

"A gift has to be cheerfully given, Lester, or it's no gift at all," I said. I suddenly felt the urge to go to the bathroom again and sprang out of bed.

Lester backed away. "Don't contaminate me! I'll do it! I'll do it!"

This time after I'd used the toilet, I brushed my teeth, then my hair. My face looked all flushed, and there were pillow creases on my cheek. I tried to smile at myself in the mirror to be sure it was me. My braces gleamed back at me. It was me, all right. But in five more months I'd be driving, I told myself. In five more months I'd have my license. And suddenly I felt a whole lot better.

By nine that evening I felt good enough to sit at my computer for twenty minutes and answer e-mails. There was a message from Pamela, another from Patrick, both telling me they hoped I was feeling better. Karen, of course, had to tell me the latest news, and I was surprised to hear that Lori and Leslie were back together.

Me: How did it happen?

Karen: Leslie wanted to test herself one last time, she told Lori. See if she had any feelings for boys.

Me: And?

Karen: She said that if ever a guy was going to appeal to her, this guy was it.

Me: So did he put the moves on her or what?

Karen: No, but all the while she was out with him, she was thinking of Lori. When she's with Lori, she said, she's "home."

When Dad came upstairs again, I told him about Lori and Leslie.

"If I turned out to be a lesbian, would you be upset?" I asked him.

He didn't answer right away. "My first thought would be that you might have a pretty rough road ahead of you. I'd want to be sure that you weren't just mixed up about your sexuality or that something hadn't happened to turn you off boys. But I wouldn't try to change you, if that's what you're asking."

I smiled up at him. "How did you get to be so wise?"

He smiled back. "Wise has nothing to do with it. When you were born, I knew I was going to love you just the way you are, however you turned out to be."

"Even though I can't carry a tune?"

"Even that," he said, and grinned.

I knew I couldn't go to school the next day because my insides still felt unsettled, and I sure didn't want to have an embarrassing accident there. It was sort of nice in a way to have the house to myself for a whole day. I took a shower, washed my hair, and even polished my nails, Rusty Rose, just as they'd been for the wedding.

By noon I felt well enough to eat some soup Sylvia had left for me. And when that didn't send me to the bathroom, I ate a banana and some crackers, then lay down on the couch to listen to a new CD Dad had brought me from the store. I must have dozed off, because the next thing I knew, the music was over, and someone was tapping on the window.

I opened my eyes and stared at the ceiling. Someone was on the porch, rapping on the window behind my head! I wanted to roll off the couch and go crawl under the dining-room table on my hands and knees, but I knew that whoever it was had seen me. Swinging my legs off the couch, I glanced around, and there was Sam Mayer from school.

He grinned through the glass and held up a copy of *The Edge*, just off the press, our last issue before winter break. I had no choice but to go to the door and let him in—me in an old pair of flannel pajamas. I hadn't even brushed my teeth after eating and probably had cracker crumbs stuck in my braces.

Sliding my tongue over my teeth, I walked out into the hall and opened the door a crack.

"I'm contagious as anything," I said, covering my mouth with one hand.

He just grinned and poked his head inside. "I'm immune. Had it last week. How you feeling?"

"A little better."

"Can I come in for a few minutes? I just wanted to bring you a copy of the paper."

"Thanks, Sam. I look a mess," I said, but I opened the door for him, and he followed me into the living room. I grabbed my robe from off a chair and threw it around me.

"You're not planning to be sick at Christmas, are you?" he joked.

"Ha! I'll still be wrapping presents Christmas morning, I'll bet," I told him. "It sure put a damper on shopping."

He looked around. "No tree?"

"We're going to get ours tonight. Dad will, anyway."

We sat down on opposite ends of the couch. "Last year, when I was going with Jennifer, she invited me over on Christmas Eve, when her family opens their presents," Sam said. "There were piles of presents! Stacks of presents! And they opened them one at a time. I almost fell asleep. It took the whole evening!"

I laughed.

"Hanukkah's a lot easier," he said. "One present per kid per night."

"How did the paper come out this time?" I asked, reaching for it and giving each page a quick glance. "Tony wanted to draw a sports cartoon for each issue. Was it any good?"

In answer, Sam pointed to the last page. In a box near the bottom there was a drawing of a heap of football players, all piled on top of each other. And off to one side a small quarterback was holding the football and saying, *"You guys looking for something?"*

I studied the cartoon, then looked at Sam. He was grinning again. "Yeah, that's what *we* thought," he said. "Tony's got to get better than that or we're going to have to pull it." He reached over and jiggled my knee with his hand. "Miss Ames said she'd like to see more in-depth articles by the staff, and she particularly mentioned that three-part series you did last spring on being part of the stage crew for *Fiddler*. What did you call it? 'Behind the Scenes of a School Production' or something? So Jayne asked each of us to come up with a half-page article on any subject we wanted. She may not use them all, but it's our next assignment."

"Could be interesting!" I said. "What are you going to write about?"

"I don't know. How it feels to break up with someone, maybe."

"You *wouldn't*!"

"Oh, I wouldn't make it personal. I wouldn't mention Jennifer or anything. Just how it feels to end a relationship. Lost love, Romeo and Juliet, that sort of thing." He smiled and stood up. "Hope you're feeling better in a few days."

"Thanks, Sam." I followed him to the door. "And if I don't see you before January, Happy New Year."

He brushed my cheek with one hand. "Take care," he said, and went out.

"Are you sure you don't want to go with us?" Sylvia asked me that night when she and Dad were discussing where to buy our tree.

"I think I'd better stay in. I still feel rumblings," I said. But I was pleased I'd been invited.

"Then what kind of tree shall we get?" Sylvia asked, pulling on a fake fur hat that looked like a white halo around her face. "Your choice."

"Well, I've always wanted a white tree. One that

looks like it's covered with snow," I told her.

"Then a white tree we shall have!" said Sylvia, looking at Dad. "We can stop at the hardware store on the way back and pick up a couple cans of that snow flocking."

I don't know if they liked my idea or not. Dad likes the natural look of things, but I figured I ought to have some say in Christmas, even though it was their first as husband and wife.

While they were gone, I made a big pot of hot chocolate and microwaved some popcorn that I kept warm in the oven. I cleaned out the corner in the living room where we usually put the tree and got down the decorations from the storage cupboard.

That about did me in—I didn't have as much energy as I'd thought—but it was a good evening. I didn't do much decorating because I still felt sort of yucky and weak, but it was fun to sit in Dad's easy chair in my robe and pajamas and give directions.

"A little to the left," I told Sylvia as she held the tree upright in one gloved hand. "Now a little toward the closet—more toward the door . . . oops, too much. . . . !" All the while Dad, on his hands and knees below, wrestled the trunk into the holder and fastened the screws.

The nice thing about Sylvia is she just throws

herself into whatever she's doing. She makes it fun. In the past Dad would always get irritated if he couldn't get the tree to stand straight, but with Sylvia there, laughing and clowning around, we had Dad laughing too, and it wasn't long before the tree was straight, the branches were sprayed, and we were sitting around eating popcorn and drinking hot chocolate before starting with the lights and ornaments.

We decided to go all blue and silver this year. So while I removed all the red and yellow and green bulbs from our string of lights and replaced them with blue, Dad and Sylvia went through the box of ornaments, selecting the silver and blue ones, then wound the string of lights around the tree.

When it was finished, we turned out the lamps and, with "White Christmas" playing on the CD player, sat together on the couch—me in the middle this time—and studied our masterpiece. I wouldn't say it was the most artfully decorated tree in the world—we didn't have enough silver ornaments, for one thing—but at least we did it as a family and for once, I was included.

On Thursday, I felt well enough to go to the shops on Georgia Avenue for a few last-minute gifts. I already had a pair of small opal earrings for Sylvia, a Greek sailor cap for Dad, and a beer cookbook for Lester. What I didn't have were the funny little toys we put in each other's stockings on Christmas morning, the wind-up kind—a hopping kangaroo or something. I wouldn't have to go all the way to the mall for those.

The bank building on the corner has a huge tree in the foyer at Christmas, and there are envelopes on the tree, each with the name of a needy child. Inside each envelope there's a letter from that kid to Santa saying what he or she most wants for Christmas. People and organizations choose an envelope, buy something for the child, then wrap it and place it under the bank's tree, with the envelope attached, so it can be delivered on Christmas Eve.

Dad and I usually stopped in and chose an envelope each year, then shopped for a gift, wrapped it, and put it under the tree. This time I went alone, looking at the names in childish scrawl. I was attracted to an envelope marked *Becky,* each letter printed in a different color. I opened the envelope.

> Dear Santa,
> You can bring me whatever you want.
> I think you are nice.
> Becky
> Age 5

I smiled and tucked her letter and envelope in my jacket pocket, then walked to the shops on the next block.

Stores often have fun presents to buy near their cash registers—wind-up spiders that race up walls, snowmen with little clocks in their bellies, plastic ice cubes with flies embedded in them. But as I was leaving one store I saw among the stuffed animals a little brown monkey that suddenly made me stop.

The monkey at home on my bed and a stuffed bear I used to have are the earliest toys I remember, but the monkey was my favorite because I could feed it from a bottle and the water would come out a hole in its bottom.

And suddenly I had this memory of Mom cutting little diapers for my monkey out of old dishtowels. I hadn't thought of that for so long, but now I could almost see us standing together at the kitchen table while she cut out little squares of cloth with pinking shears, then pinned one around the monkey's bottom.

Some things I hardly remember about my mother at all, but that memory is as clear as anything. I looked at the price on the monkey—a lot more than I felt I could afford—but I bought it anyway, and the girl behind the counter gift wrapped it for me.

I taped Becky's envelope to the package and went back to the bank to place it under the tree.

Dad and Sylvia went to the Messiah Sing-Along at our church that night, but I stayed home to wrap presents. I put on all my favorite carols while I wrapped and enjoyed the lights on the tree.

It really *was* beginning to feel like Christmas at our place. I had even begun to feel that we were a real family, especially the next day when Sylvia and I spent the whole day in the kitchen together baking: Swedish butter cookies, pecan rounds, peanut butter fudge, chocolate roll-ups.

When Dad came home, we cut fresh holly from our bush in the backyard and decorated our mantel. We were going to have a special candle-light dinner on Christmas Eve before we went to church—Dad and Sylvia and Lester and me—and on Christmas afternoon one of Lester's roommates, Paul Sorenson, was coming over for Christmas dinner. Our whole house seemed brighter, livelier, busier, merrier with Sylvia around. Dad looked so much younger, I couldn't get over it. I'd have to say that Sylvia Summers was one of the best things that ever happened to him.

On Christmas Eve morning I got up early, feeling the best I had all week, and set about whipping up eggs to scramble. But when Dad came down-stairs, he said, "Don't make any for Sylvia, Al. I'm afraid she's got the same thing you had. She spent half the night in the bathroom."

I stared. "She's sick? It's the day before Christmas!"

"I know," said Dad.

I thought of the candlelight dinner we'd planned. The service at church. Lester coming over Christmas morning and Paul joining us that afternoon. I thought of the gifts and the fudge and the . . .

"What are we going to do?" I said, still holding the frying pan in one hand.

"We'll just have to delay Christmas," said Dad.

16

Caring for Sylvia

I can honestly say that my first thought was not that Sylvia was ruining Christmas, but how sad it was that she was sick on the first Christmas she and Dad would spend together as husband and wife. And I knew exactly what she was going through when I heard her rushing footsteps in the hall, the close of the bathroom door, and the flush of the toilet—a second and a third time.

"Al," Dad said before he left for work, "this is going to be one of the busiest days at the store. We're closing early, but until then I just have to be there. I'm going to count on you to take care of Sylvia, but I want you to call me if you think she's getting worse."

"I can do it, Dad. Don't worry," I told him.

He kissed my forehead and went out to the car. I saw him look up toward their bedroom window and knew he'd rather be here taking care of Sylvia than anywhere else in the world.

I went up to my room and waited till Sylvia was back in hers. Then I tapped on her door. "Sylvia?"

"Yes?" came her weak voice.

I opened the door just a crack. "Can I come in a minute?"

"Sure."

All I could see was a lump under the covers.

"I know just how you feel," I said.

"Only I had to go and get sick at Christmas, with everyone invited for dinner," she said.

"Well, as Dad says, we're simply postponing Christmas," I told her. "Now what can I get you? Anything at all?"

"Some ginger ale later, maybe," she said.

"Just let me know," I said, and went back downstairs.

I did the breakfast dishes, picked up magazines and things in the living room, folded the morning paper. It occurred to me suddenly that Christmas this year would sort of be up to me. Dad was working, Les was probably doing last-minute shopping, Sylvia was sick, and I was in charge.

I decided to set the table for our first holiday meal, whenever it might be. So I put on our best tablecloth and napkins, the centerpiece we used each Christmas—a bouquet of small red felt reindeer that look like red flowers from a distance—and the snowmen-shaped salt and pepper shakers that Lester gave Mom when he was ten. I hung the twirling red-and-gold paper swirl decoration from the light fixture over the table, so that it dangled, glistening, and I sorted through our Christmas CDs to find the ones by the Mormon Tabernacle Choir and the Choir of King's College and the Robert Shaw Chorale. We've played those for as long as I can remember.

Upstairs the toilet flushed again, and I wondered if Sylvia was dizzy like I had been. I went to check. She was back in her room. There weren't any soiled pajama bottoms on the bathroom floor that I could wash for her, but the toilet bowl was splattered, and I cleaned it up. As I was putting the brush away, I thought that maybe this is what being a family is all about—being able to be yourself without apologizing. You just are. You just *be*. Be sick, and your family accepts you.

Dad called at noon, and I told him I thought Sylvia was sleeping. The next time I went upstairs, I took her an ice bag and a glass of ginger ale. I was placing them on her nightstand when Sylvia came back from the bathroom.

"Do I look as bad as I feel?" she asked, her lips dry and cracked-looking.

"You look exactly like you're supposed to look when you're sick," I said, and she gave a little laugh. She lay down on the bed but didn't pull the

covers up. "I'm so warm, and I ache all over. That's a symptom of flu, isn't it? My arms, my legs, my shoulders . . ."

"Let me give you a back rub," I said, and sat down on the edge of the bed.

She glanced over at me, and I felt sure I'd gotten much too personal, but I was surprised to hear her say, "*Would* you, Alice? I can't think of anything I'd like more." She turned away from me then, on her side, and unbuttoned the front of her pajama top so it slid halfway down her back and shoulders.

I gently massaged her neck, then moved down to her shoulders and back, remembering how achy I had felt, not rubbing too hard. I could tell by the way her body relaxed under my palms that I must be doing it right.

"Oh, that feels so good," she said. "Right now I hardly have the strength to move, but if I had a tail, Alice, it would wag to thank you."

We both laughed then.

"Dad called to see how you are," I said. "I told him you were sleeping. He said to tell you he's stopping at a diner and bringing home some split pea soup for dinner, that you're not to lift a finger till you're better."

"That's why I married that man," said Sylvia. "He's the most considerate guy in the world,

Alice. I never knew a man who was kinder. I wonder how many others would wait a year for me to make up my mind and then wait another three months while I took care of my sister. He came into my life at exactly the right time. And look what I got! You and Lester, too! Three for the price of one!"

I smiled and, as an extra bonus, got some lotion from my dresser and rubbed it onto her back and shoulders. Then I pulled the sheet over her and told her to sleep.

Lester called around three. "So what are we doing tonight?" he asked. "Dad left a message that Sylvia has the flu."

"Yeah, and you and Dad are probably next in line," I told him.

"Well, you're Little Miss Sunshine, aren't you?" he said.

"We're just going to celebrate Christmas when everyone's up to it," I told him.

"Oh," said Lester. And then, after a pause, "so if I wanted to take in a movie, that would be okay?"

"Perfectly," I told him. "Unless you want to eat pea soup with us."

"I'll pass," said Lester. "Check in with you again tomorrow."

Sylvia came downstairs to eat pea soup with us

around seven, but none of us went to the midnight service at church. Instead, I lit the Christmas candles in the windows and a fire in the fireplace, and then I turned off all the lights except those on the tree. Sylvia lay on the couch, her head in Dad's lap, as we watched the sparkles on the tree, shadows dancing on the walls, and listened to a CD Dad had brought home of handbells playing carols.

"You know," Sylvia said around nine, "I may be feeling better. I think I might be able to cook dinner tomorrow night."

"I'll help!" I said.

"We won't make any decision till tomorrow," said Dad. "We'll see how you feel in the morning. But I'm going to make breakfast for anyone who cares to come to the table—pecan pancakes, my specialty."

After Sylvia went to bed, Dad and I slipped the funny presents we'd bought into the four stockings we hung from the mantel. And the next morning, as promised, Dad was in the kitchen making his famous pancakes, and there was Lester at the table. We'd sort of skipped Christmas Eve this year and jumped right into Christmas Day, but that was all right. It would have been all right if it had been a couple days later or even a week, because what was important was that we were all here together.

* * *

Sylvia spent Christmas morning in her robe and pajamas. She didn't eat any pancakes, but she squeezed orange juice for the rest of us and looked as though she really did feel much better. We gathered around the tree about eleven to open our gifts. I seemed to have chosen well, because Dad looked great in his sailor cap, Sylvia loved her opal earrings, and Lester declared he would try one of the cooking-with-beer recipes on his friends.

The way Lester presented his gift to me was a surprise. It came in a package half the size of a shoe box, and when I opened it, I found a miniature Mercedes Benz.

"Oh, Les!" I joked. "I've always dreamed of owning a Mercedes."

He grinned. "It's a 1936 convertible," he said. "Open the hood." I did. There was a tightly rolled twenty-dollar bill attached to a slip of paper that read, *This certificate entitles Alice McKinley to six driving lessons or as many as it takes her to get her license. The twenty she can use however she likes.*

I reached across the couch and hugged him. "There," I said. "You just got my germs if I have any left."

Sylvia had knitted a sweater for me—a really neat green sweater with a sort of ruffled edge on each cuff and around the boat neckline.

"It's gorgeous!" I said. "When in the world did you have time to make it, Sylvia?"

"While I was in New Mexico taking care of Nancy," she explained. "It helped keep my mind off her, so I called it my 'lifesaver sweater.'"

"I'll call it my 'lifetime sweater'! I'll wear it forever!" I declared, and hugged her, too.

It was Dad's present that really shocked me, though. It was wrapped in birthday paper, because he always picks up the first roll of paper he finds in the closet. Sometimes it says HAPPY ANNIVERSARY on it, and once he even gave me a present wrapped in Father's Day paper.

I opened the lid of the box. Inside was a little silver cell phone.

"Dad!" I said. "I don't believe this! I didn't think you'd ever let me have a phone of my own!"

"Well, Sylvia convinced me it was time," he said. "After you went out with that Tony boy on Halloween and I told you to call if you needed me, I realized you couldn't call if you weren't near a phone, and I figured a cell phone was the way to go. I *do* hope you'll reserve it for important calls, though."

"Yeah, Al. Don't be one of those people on the bus who calls a friend and tells her every street she's passing," said Lester.

"Or everything she ate for dinner," said Sylvia.

"Or every store you're going to stop in at the mall," said Dad.

"I won't!" I said excitedly, knowing that I would call every single friend I had, though, and give them my cell phone number.

We had our Christmas dinner around seven that night. Sylvia dressed and did a rib roast, and the rest of us pitched in and cooked everything else. Paul Sorenson came, bringing a chocolate silk pie for dessert. He was a tall, thin guy, taller and leaner than Lester, and far more serious, it seemed—at least around our table. He looked to me as though he could be majoring in chemistry or geology or something dry and academic, not exactly the type of guy Pamela or Elizabeth would go nuts over. But I could tell that Dad liked him, that he was glad Lester was rooming with somebody responsible and mature.

I was right about his major.

"What are you studying, Paul?" Dad asked as the roast went around the table a second time, followed by the garlic mashed potatoes.

"Geology," Paul said, and I couldn't help myself. I laughed out loud, and everyone looked at me.

"Oops! Sorry!" I said. "It's just that I guessed . . ."

Lester can read me like a book. "He also is a part-time dance instructor and plays bluegrass," he said.

We all laughed then, even Paul. What is it they say—you can't tell a book by its cover?

"So what's George Palamas like, then?" I asked about the third guy in their apartment.

"Majored in business and listens to Bach," said Lester, and now we *did* laugh.

"It was a good dinner, Sylvia," I told her later when we went to the kitchen to serve the pie.

She smiled. "And to think I made it all through dinner without going to the bathroom once."

The rest of us did the dishes and cleaned up the dining room while Sylvia stretched out on the couch. We put all the wrapping paper in the trash, started a fire in the fireplace, and after Lester and Paul said good-bye, I sat in a chair across from Sylvia, wondering if the little girl named Becky liked the brown monkey I had bought for her. Wondering too about Latisha, an angry little girl I'd counseled at camp last summer. I guess I hadn't noticed Sylvia get up and go upstairs, but when she came down again, she was carrying another present. She sat down on the couch and patted the cushion beside her.

"Come sit by me, Alice," she said. "I have one more gift for you. It's not finished, of course, and I don't think I'll ever really get it done . . ."

I couldn't imagine what it could be. I got up and

went over, wondering if she meant she'd been embroidering something for *my* wedding, should I ever marry.

"Do you know what it is?" I asked Dad.

"Haven't the faintest," he said, settling back with a glass of wine.

It was about fifteen inches square, two inches thick, and I took off the wrapping paper to find a scrapbook that had obviously been hand-covered in tightly stretched blue gingham.

Curiously, I turned to the first page, and there was a typed copy of a poem:

> *There is a lady sweet and kind,*
> *Was never face so pleased my mind;*
> *I did but see her passing by,*
> *And yet I love her till I die.*

> *Her gesture, motion, and her smiles,*
> *Her wit, her voice, my heart beguiles.*
> *Beguiles my heart, I know not why,*
> *And yet I love her till I die.*

> *Cupid is wingèd and doth range,*
> *Her country so my love doth change:*
> *But change she earth, or change she sky,*
> *Yet will I love her till I die.*

I stared. I couldn't believe she'd remembered it. When I was in Miss Summers's seventh-grade English class and believing she was the wisest and most beautiful woman I'd ever seen—the nicest, anyway—she had assigned us to choose a poem that really meant something to us, memorize it, and recite it to the class with feeling. A poem that expressed something about ourselves.

I had found a poetry book of Mom's on our shelf, with notations in her handwriting in the margins. I'd memorized a portion of one of her favorite poems, *Thanatopsis,* because I'd hoped it would make me feel closer to the mother I couldn't remember as well as I'd wanted.

But in going through the book, I'd found another poem that had caught my eye, and every time I worked at remembering the first poem, I'd stop and read the second.

And on that particular day, the day I was supposed to recite *Thanatopsis,* about death, I realized I was reciting a poem instead about a woman I'd love forever—my mom, of course—and . . . and I started crying. Right there in front of the class. And I remembered how kind Sylvia was about it. I looked over at her now, sitting beside me.

"I think that's when I started loving you," she said.

"*You* started loving *me*?" I said, astonished.

She nodded. "I kept that poem—I copied it out of a poetry book of my own—and put it in your student folder," she said.

I turned to the next page, and there was a picture of me sitting at my desk at school, smiling.

"Remember how I took pictures of each of you the first day of class? I always take photos of my students and keep them in their folders. It helps me associate faces with names," she explained.

There was an essay I'd written about my father and also an assignment we'd done on personality, where I'd associated all my family members with characters from musicals—Dad, I remember, was "The Music Man," Lester was "Li'l Abner," Mom was "Funny Girl," and I was "Annie." There was a program from the Messiah Sing-Along when Sylvia first met my father, the ribbon off the first gift I'd given her. . . . She, Sylvia Summers, the teacher I had worshipped all those years, had been keeping a scrapbook of *me*!

Only half the book was full. The rest of the pages were blank.

"If you'll let me be the keeper of the scrapbook, Alice, I'd like to finish it myself with things I would like to remember about you," she said.

I guess even if you don't grow in someone's body, you can grow in someone's heart. They say that before you are conceived, you are just a gleam

in your father's eye. I guess you can also be a picture in somebody's scrapbook. I had just found out that even before Miss Summers knew she would marry my dad—before she'd even met him—she had liked me and thought I was special.

I closed the book and handed it back to her. "Yes," I said.

She looked at me questioningly for a moment.

"Yes, you can keep it," I said. I put my arms around her and whispered, "I always loved you too. Even before you knew it."

17

A New Year

Everyone seemed to be busy on New Year's Eve. I was hoping that Gwen and Elizabeth and Pamela and I could spend the night at one of our houses, but Gwen's family goes to church on New Year's Eve; Elizabeth had agreed to baby-sit her little brother so that her folks could go out, and she's not allowed to have friends in when she baby-sits. Pamela was going to be at her mother's.

"I have to," she explained. "I spent Christmas with Dad, so I've got to spend New Year's Eve with her. It's called 'appeasement.'"

Elizabeth and I looked at her sympathetically. We were in Pamela's bedroom, after spending a day at the mall looking for post-Christmas bargains. Pamela rolled over on her back, holding a pillow to her chest. "To tell the truth," she went on, "I figure if I'm with her, at least she won't go

for about a year, and this time I'm going to hold him to it."

When Dad came out of the bathroom all showered and shaven, he stopped in his tracks and looked at Sylvia. Then he buttoned the cuffs of his shirt and gave a low whistle. "Ummm. We could, you know, stay home," he teased.

"Not a chance. You promised me dancing," she told him.

I smiled to myself. That was his first surprise of the evening. When they got home later, he'd discover she had on black lace underwear. I knew, because I'd zipped her up.

They were going to dinner first, so they left around eight. I promised myself I would *not* sit around sulking. I would read magazines and eat fudge and play CDs and have a good time all by myself and . . .

The phone rang.

Ha! I smiled. *Just like in the movies!* My first thought was that Patrick and his folks had come home early from New Hampshire and he wanted to spend New Year's Eve with me. Or maybe it was Eric calling from Texas, and never mind Emily.

"Hello?" I said.

"Hey! Whatcha doin'?" said Lester.

He could probably hear the disappointment in my voice. I had secretly hoped it might even be

has always looked out for number one, don't you worry."

We spent the rest of the afternoon calling all our friends to see what the other kids were doing. Penny was going to a party at a neighbor's, Karen's mom had invited relatives, Brian was going to a party, and so was Mark.

"I think I'll just go to bed at eight o'clock, pull the covers up over my head, and enjoy my aching teeth," I told Pamela and Elizabeth before I went home. "See you next year."

My teeth did hurt too. They're close together, and every time the orthodontist tightens the bands, it's murder. But I guess there are a lot worse things that can happen to you. At least I had teeth.

That evening I helped Sylvia get dressed. She was wearing a short black dress with a low neckline, and when I zipped her up in back, she hardly had room to wiggle.

"Wow, Sylvia!" I said, watching her slip on high-heeled sling-back shoes. "You're going to give my dad a heart attack!"

She giggled as she put on dangling earrings of pearl and rhinestone clusters and I fastened the clasp on her necklace. "Have I overdone it?" she asked. "He's been promising to take me dancing

for about a year, and this time I'm going to hold him to it."

When Dad came out of the bathroom all showered and shaven, he stopped in his tracks and looked at Sylvia. Then he buttoned the cuffs of his shirt and gave a low whistle. "Ummm. We could, you know, stay home," he teased.

"Not a chance. You promised me dancing," she told him.

I smiled to myself. That was his first surprise of the evening. When they got home later, he'd discover she had on black lace underwear. I knew, because I'd zipped her up.

They were going to dinner first, so they left around eight. I promised myself I would *not* sit around sulking. I would read magazines and eat fudge and play CDs and have a good time all by myself and . . .

The phone rang.

Ha! I smiled. *Just like in the movies!* My first thought was that Patrick and his folks had come home early from New Hampshire and he wanted to spend New Year's Eve with me. Or maybe it was Eric calling from Texas, and never mind Emily.

"Hello?" I said.

"Hey! Whatcha doin'?" said Lester.

He could probably hear the disappointment in my voice. I had secretly hoped it might even be

Sam Mayer. I wasn't in the mood to listen to Lester talk about a gorgeous new babe he was taking out that night.

"If you want the truth, nothing," I said.

"No kidding? Well, I've got some people coming over for the evening, and I wondered if you'd like to come too."

I could not believe what I was hearing. It was eight thirty on New Year's Eve, and my brother—my twenty-three-year-old *brother*—was inviting *me* to his party on New Year's Eve?

"What?" I cried.

"What don't you understand?" said Lester. "P-A-R-T-Y."

"Well . . . sure!" I said. "But Dad and Sylvia have already left and—"

"George'll be over in about a half hour to pick you up, okay?"

"Les, what shall I wear?"

"You're naked?"

"No, I'm not naked! I've got on jeans and a shirt."

"That's fine. See you soon," said Lester, and hung up.

Oh no! I thought. I wasn't going to Lester's looking like a kid sister. I remembered when I'd gone to a lingerie shower for Crystal Harkins before she married and felt out of place the whole evening.

That wasn't going to happen again. I knew how a woman was supposed to look on New Year's Eve. I'd seen how Sylvia looked, hadn't I? What should it be? The bridesmaid dress I'd worn for Crystal's wedding? It was probably a little too tight now across the chest. The dress I'd worn for Sylvia's wedding?

I ran upstairs and pulled out the backless slip dress I'd worn when Lester took me to the *Tony 'n' Tina's Wedding* show for my fifteenth birthday. Yanking off my clothes, I put on fresh makeup, fresh deodorant, and then remembered I couldn't wear a bra with that dress, and my breasts were a little larger than they'd been in May. So what? I said. If models went without bras, I could too.

The problem was, I was freezing. It had been spring when we'd gone to *Tony 'n' Tina's Wedding,* and this was December. I pulled on a pair of panty hose and the beige flats with crisscross straps that I'd worn with this dress before. Then I stood in front of the mirror.

Oh my God! The dress was a little tight across the stomach! I looked pregnant! And what would I wear for a coat? I grabbed a fleece jacket and got downstairs just as a car turned in our driveway.

When I stepped out on the porch, I saw snowflakes just beginning to fall, floating lazily down in front of the headlights. A stocky man got out.

"Alice?" he said. "Hi! I'm George. Crawl in the backseat there, and Joan and I will drop you off."

I got in back and could smell the woman's perfume before I even closed the door. Her face was barely visible, but her earrings sparkled and I was glad I had put on my sparkly earrings too.

"Hi," she said. "You're Les's sister?"

"Yes."

George got in and backed out of the drive. "The guys drew straws to see who had to stay home for Mr. Watts on New Year's Eve, and Les got the short straw. He decided to invite some people in and wants you to help keep him company."

I laughed. "Okay."

"Aren't you freezing?" Joan asked me.

"No, really, I'm fine," I said, and wondered if she could hear my teeth chattering.

We talked about what a good deal it was for George and Paul and Lester to share their great apartment rent-free as long as they did jobs about the place for Mr. Watts.

And then the car pulled in the driveway of the big Victorian house, and George said, "Have a good time, now."

They weren't going in, then. I wondered who was going to drive me back home if George and his girlfriend were going out for the evening. But I

was too cold to think about that now, so I ran up the side steps and knocked.

I could hear voices and laughter and music coming from inside, and I realized no one could hear my knock, so I just opened the door and went in. I took off the fleece jacket in the hallway so I could make a proper entrance and walked into a roomful of people sitting around in jeans and sweaters and their stocking feet. They all stopped talking and looked at me, and suddenly Lester leaped up out of his chair.

"Hey, everyone, this is Alice. She's just come from a party and she's freezing, so I'll introduce her around after we get her in warmer clothes," he said.

Before I could even open my mouth, I felt his arm around my shoulders, steering me out of the living room and into his bedroom across the hall.

"Lester!" I choked. "I didn't *bring* any other clothes! I thought this was a New Year's Eve party!"

"*I* thought I told you to come as you were!" he said. "*Look* at you!"

I was standing in front of Lester's mirror, so I looked, and the fact that I was cold, I guess, made my nipples stand out even more. It looked as though I had two pencil erasers stuck under the front of my dress. I could have died of embarrassment.

"Okay," Lester said, opening his closet door.

"You can sit around in my bathrobe all evening or—"

"No!" I cried.

"Then put on these." Lester threw a pair of his
jeans on the bed, a belt, a black turtleneck, a ski
sweater, and a pair of wool socks.

"Come on out when you're dressed," he said,
and went back to the party.

I felt like crying, but I wouldn't let myself. I took
off my dress and panty hose and shoes and pulled
on Lester's jeans, which were about eight inches
too long and eight inches too wide around the
waist. But there were goose bumps all over my
arms, so the turtleneck felt delicious sliding down
over my body, thick with Lester's scent. I rolled up
the bottoms of the jeans and was able to pull his
belt just tight enough to keep the pants up. Then
I put on the wool socks and finally the sweater,
which had a row of pine trees woven across the
front. The striped socks on my feet looked like
something out of a Dr. Seuss book, but boy, was I
warm and comfortable!

I gave my hair a few licks with Lester's brush as
I looked around his room. He had the same size
bed as Dad and Sylvia's, a chest of drawers, a computer table in one corner, a desk in another, and
bookshelves all over the place.

It was time to join the party, and I took a deep

breath. I would not let my goof spoil the evening, I told myself. Lester had covered for me, and now here I was, in my brother's apartment, in my brother's clothes, and I was going to enjoy myself.

I padded out to the living room and saw Lester grin at me from across the room. I sat down on the rug in front of his chair while he introduced me to the others: a married couple with a new baby in an infant seat; two women who worked in the registrar's office at the university; and a couple of men and a third woman who were class-mates of Lester's.

The strange thing was, none of the women appeared to be Lester's "significant other." None of them even looked "romantically inclined" toward him. They just all appeared to be good friends, happy to be together on the last night of the year.

And suddenly I knew what I was going to write about for the newspaper; I thought maybe I'd title it "Who Says?"

Who was it, I'd write, who tells the rest of us what we should do or be or feel? Who says that we are supposed to dress up on New Year's Eve and that if you're not with one special person, you're a nobody? Come to think of it, who says that everyone has to rise when the bride comes down the aisle? That she has to have a diamond engage-ment ring or that the groom has to wear a tux?

That you have to eat turkey on Thanksgiving, or wear a certain brand of jeans, or have your braces off before you're fifteen? Who says?

Here I was in clothes several sizes too big, not a boyfriend in sight, sitting here with no one I'd ever met before except my brother, and I was happier than a bug in a rug.

The newborn in the infant seat squirmed and scrunched up his face as though he might cry, but his mother said it was only a gas bubble.

"Would you like to hold him?" she said, smiling at me as I leaned over her baby.

"Sure!" I said, and she handed me his tiny warm body, hardly heavier than a kitten.

As I felt him squirm against me, I remembered a time back in fourth grade when I'd held a teacher's baby against my shoulder—Mr. Dooley's baby—and he had burped. I patted the little body I was holding now as his parents watched approvingly, and thought how he didn't know anything about all the "shoulds." All he had to do was be himself, and he was accepted just as he was. And so should I be accepted for being me. So should Lori and Leslie, just as they were. So should Amy Sheldon and David, if he decided to be a priest.

The baby burped, and I handed him back to his father as everyone clapped.

"She's got the magic touch," said the mother.

The phone rang just then, and Lester went to the kitchen to answer. When he came back he said, "That was Mr. Watts downstairs. He wanted to wish us all a Happy New Year, and he says if we want to turn up the music, it's okay with him, because he's taking out his hearing aid and going to bed."

We laughed and one of the men offered a toast to Mr. Watts and his wonderful house.

"I called home and left a message on the answering machine in case Dad and Sylvia get home first and wonder where you are," Lester told me as people circled the table, filling their plates with tacos and chips.

That meant I could stay as long as I wanted! That I was part of the group. I belonged. I'd forgotten all about my braces. In fact, I'd smiled with my lips apart and hadn't even thought about it.

"Thanks for inviting me, Les," I said.

"Hey, *some*body's got to stick around and help with the dishes, right?" he said, and gave my shoulder a squeeze.

The evening went so fast—just talking and listening to music and holding the baby and eating—that we were surprised when someone said it was midnight.

We could hear horns honking down the road and fireworks going off in the distance. I went to a window and saw snowflakes drifting down in the light of a streetlamp. The tops of cars were dusted with white.

"Hey, everyone! It's still snowing!" I said. "That just about makes it perfect!"

Lester opened the French doors at the back of the apartment, and we all stepped out on the upstairs porch to welcome in a new year.